She looked at the two women.

"Your husband is in the same warehouse he was in before I was attacked. I don't know who's holding him."

Beth sank down into herself as if completely defeated.

Sarah asked, "Isn't there something else we can do? We really need information."

"Even if I had been able to find him, I still would need to go in with the men. They might move him again. They might have used a decoy to trick anyone searching for him. I can be fooled. Roosevelt's and Morrigu's magics are both powerful and deep."

A thought was coming to her, niggling at her consciousness, but it was lost, when Beth asked, "When can you go?"

"When will the others be ready?"

"Tonight," said Beth.

"I can be ready tonight," she said.

RESCUE MISSION

ALSO BY LINDA JORDAN:

Explosive Resistance: Islands of Seattle, Book 2

Battle Magic: Islands of Seattle, Book 3

Warriors Rising: Islands of Seattle, Book 4

Divine War: Islands of Seattle, Book 5

Notes on the Moon People

Infected by Magic

Faerie Unraveled: The Bones of the Earth Series, Book 1

Faerie Contact: The Bones of the Earth Series, Book 2

Faerie Descent: The Bones of the Earth Series, Book 3

Faerie Flight: The Bones of the Earth Series, Book 4

Faerie Confluence: The Bones of the Earth Series, Book 5

Come on over to Linda's website and join the fun!

LindaJordan.net

Don't miss a release!

Sign up for Linda's Serendipitous Newsletter while you're there.

RESCUE MISSION

ISLANDS OF SEATTLE, BOOK 1

LINDA JORDAN

Welcome to the Islands Christine

Linda Jordan

METAMORPHOSIS PRESS

Published by Metamorphosis Press

www.MetamorphosisPress.com

ISBN 13: 978-1946914064

For Michael & Zoe

CADY

CADY WAS A FINDER. THE GIFT RAN THROUGH HER BLOOD. Either from her father, whoever he was, or her mom. Mom died from the flu, when Cady was only five.

Cady never found out who her people were or what powers they had. The people who cared for her didn't talk about magic. It was evil to them. Both talking about it and using it.

She had been born all wrong. Mom hadn't made it to the hospital. The neighbor's mules had been pulling the cart, but with all the rain it got stuck in the mud of the new road. Hospitals were far away and scary places anyway. Not enough staff, or medicine these days. Ever since the last pandemic, things had been that way. At least that's what folks claimed.

So, Mom had given birth with the help of the neighbor and a couple of other folks who happened past. Midwives were hard to come by, especially if you didn't have money. And Mom didn't. She was a weaver and most of her work was paid for by bartering. She'd always been rich with chickens.

Cady had come out backwards and with a broken arm.

Her left arm never did heal properly and was always weaker than her right. Slightly misshapen, causing her to look off-balance, even as she'd grown up.

This morning the fingers on her bad arm tingled. A warning. Someone was coming to ask for her help.

She closed her eyes and breathed in the fresh air of dawn. It rained last night making everything smell good. The sky was clear. The sun just beginning to rise. A fine spring morning. She needed to plant today if she wanted food this spring.

The last few days she'd cleared the soil of the winter cover crop. The varied thrushes were over by her compost pile, sifting through the dead leaves and looking for insects. The sun was still low in the sky, shafts of light streamed through the leafless, big leaf maples that towered over her house.

Just there, through the stream of light, a movement. A woman, no a goddess, walked. She had long blond hair and wore a gauzy, muslin dress decorated with cherry blossoms and dandelions. Cady could see that where the goddess walked, meadowsweet in full bloom sprang up. The goddess paid no attention to Cady, of course. Intent on her own life.

Then the wind changed and Cady got a waft of her neighbor's smoke. Joe was burning his garbage again. It stank, must be something awful in there. He raised goats and sometimes burned their carcasses if they died from disease.

She closed her front door and went back inside the tiny one room building that was home. She'd always meant to add onto it and make it larger, but time or energy never put in an appearance together.

It had been built as a guest house, Cady speculated. Once upon a time, when the world had been much different. The main house had long since collapsed, its remains reused elsewhere or burnt. Probably, taken down by the Big One, like most of the other large houses in this part of the world. Her little shack hadn't been bothered much. When she'd found it twenty years ago and hacked away the forest intent on reclaiming the land, the building had some water damage. She'd patched up the leaks and added a small wood stove a neighbor had salvaged, to keep warm in the winter. The furniture that came with it, a bed frame, a wooden table and oak chair were still usable. The mattress, ruined. So she'd burned it and made a new one from some second-hand fabric; adding chicken and duck feathers that she and the other villagers plucked from birds destined for dinners. It had taken weeks to gather enough feathers.

There was a teeny bathroom, but city water was long gone, as was the actual city. What remained of Seattle was all islands. She and Joe shared a well with a solar pump. She had cold running water in the kitchen and felt blessed with that luxury. Cady used her bathtub to do laundry in, the drain had been re-plumbed with a large hose that took the gray water out to the garden. She had a composting toilet, another luxury in this part of the world. Baths, she took down at the lake.

It was a fine little home. Perfect for her.

She brushed her long, thick gray hair, then braided it and tied the tip with a strip of cloth from an old shirt. She dressed in old khaki pants, her dark leather boots and a long sleeved blue shirt.

The tea kettle on the wood stove sang and Cady poured the boiling water through the muslin bag of dried herbs and flowers. Mint, lavender and rosebuds scented the air. A lovely smell for early spring when none of those were available fresh.

She sat down at the table, her hands wrapped around the hot mug, trying to warm them. Feeling the ache in her fingers. Most of them had been broken at one time or another and even those that healed well told her it had been a cold night. She was only fifty, but arthritis had set in.

In the corner sat a bookcase stuffed with very, very old books. Some, she'd even read, opening the creaky pages. The glue in some was gone and many pages, completely unmoored. Several of the books were on gardening with photos of lavish estates, propped up by pesticides and irrigations systems that were no longer possible to use, let alone find the plumbing pieces for.

The world had changed so much since then. The flu of 2020, the polar ice caps nearly melting, and the Big One—the quake in 2032 that took out huge portion of the West Coast of North America, everything was different. In Seattle, more so than many places. But Cady heard that all of the devastation had ripple effects everywhere.

She dipped the tea bag a couple of times, then set it in a small flowered bowl which sat on the battered wooden table. Then sipped the hot tea, tasting the strong mint and lavender flavors. The rose subtly formed a background note.

Refugees had fled inland from every coastal city that drowned. What had that been like? To pick up and leave their lives behind. Entire countries were gone beneath the sea, their cultures lost. Those people had been assimilated into nearby countries. Sometimes though they'd ended up moving clear across the world. Except not in the U.S., who'd closed its borders as the pandemic spread. Too late, though. The pandemic still hit here.

The countries who took in refugees set up a trade embargo against the U.S. California got pissed off at the federal government, who wouldn't help with the double whammy of earthquake disaster and rising tides. So California split off into their own country. Washington, D.C. was too busy managing multiple crises to deal with them. Then the Western halves of Oregon and Washington joined up with British Columbia to form Cascadia.

Washington, D.C. was way too busy to even take notice of Cascadia. They were dealing with all the quakes caused by fracking in the Midwest, overcrowding everywhere, horrendous hurricanes and tornados, and flooded cities of their own.

And the water kept rising. And the weather got wilder. It was as if the entire planet had turned upside down and was trying to destroy the plague of humanity.

But there was something else. Something that no one predicted. Not a soul had even expected.

With the complete disorganization of humankind, the disruption of technology and the toppling of societal structures, magic had returned to the world.

Just the thought of that made Cady smile. Magic. Where would her world be without it?

Perhaps, it had been caused by the mingling of cultures who'd rarely spoken and now lived side by side. Perhaps, it was the world shaking up like a handful of dice. Or perhaps, the quakes and the winds stirred up things that had long lay sleeping.

One day it was an Egyptian Goddess appearing in a town. The next, a dragon swept across a field, igniting the grass. The third day it was an old white preacher damning the wicked with fire shooting out his fingertips, lighting the entire church on fire. He burned to death, a testament to his own wickedness.

The incidents went on and on. Cities fell into the sea and quakes wracked the heartland. Seattle had stabilized, at least as stable as it would ever be. The Space Needle became the Sea

Needle and the land transformed itself into the Islands of Seattle. I-5 which had once been far, far, above the water level now touched it. No one sane dared to drive on it, fearing its collapse.

Most people had already abandoned cars anyway, there was little gasoline available and its cost was dear. A few people made their own diesel, but re-used cooking oil was hard to come by because even fresh cooking oil was hard to come by and expensive.

Some people retrofitted their cars, making them run on solar power. If they had the money or skill. The roads were shot and there was no guarantee how long any structure that was ramped would stay that way, between quake damage and wet soil.

Cady's mom had lived until Cady was five, but then another round of the flu passed through and took her. Cady was raised by neighbors, passed around from family to family, until she was fifteen and old enough to be on her own. Or so she thought.

She ran away to start her own life and made so many mistakes. Then again, that led her to where she was now. So perhaps they hadn't been mistakes after all.

She sipped her tea. The flavors waking her up fully.

Time to get some breakfast and get on with her day. Get those greens and peas planted.

Monster shot in through the cat door and his black bulk streaked under the bed, as the door went kathump, kathump. He was her early warning system.

Someone was here.

Cady stood, peering out through the antique flowered curtains. She recognized Sarah, who was walking towards

Cady's house, with her arm around another woman's shoulders.

Sarah never spoke to Cady. Sarah was one of those who didn't have magic and probably didn't trust it. They were still a few of those people around. How they survived with goddesses walking through the village puzzled Cady. Something must be very wrong for Sarah to bring someone to see her.

Cady put the tea kettle on again and lit the burner.

There was a knock on the door.

She opened it.

"Cady, hello," said Sarah.

"Hi."

"Can we come in? Beth needs to sit down."

Beth, who Cady didn't recognize, had a huge belly. Obviously pregnant and the baby must have dropped. Or else this was one of a series and her body normally carried low. Cady wasn't a midwife and didn't know a lot about babies, but she listened.

"Sure, come on in."

She held the door open and closed it behind them.

The table had three chairs, Beth sat in one, breathing heavily. The woman looked ready to give birth any minute.

"Tea anyone?"

"Yes please," said Beth.

"I have mint, chamomile, raspberry leaf or summer surprise—which is all sorts of dried flowers. Rose petals, calendula, borage."

"Chamomile for me," said Beth. "No wait, better make it mint. My digestion's been awful lately. And I'm so sick of raspberry leaf tea, I don't think I could keep it down."

"I'll have summer surprise," said Sarah.

After she made tea and refilled her own, Cady sat down.

"What brings you here on this fine morning?" asked Cady, knowing it couldn't be anything good.

Beth burst into tears.

"I'm sorry," said Cady, gently touching Beth's arm. The woman vibrated chaotic energy.

"It's an awful morning. At the end of a horrible week," said Beth. Her eyes looked puffy as if she'd been crying for a day or two. Her short dark, hair was greasy and unbrushed. The woman wasn't taking care of herself.

Cady just waited, silent. Stirring the contents of her mug before removing the muslin tea bag and setting it in the bowl. Little rituals to ground herself and help her be open to whatever was coming.

Sarah repeated Cady's actions, then took the bag out of Beth's tea and added a spoonful of Joe's honey from the jar on the table. Joe also raised bees who pollinated the plants in Cady's garden, for which she was grateful, even without the honey that frequently came her way.

Beth wiped her face and said, "I'm sorry. I'm not usually like this, but this pregnancy has been really hard. And then Monday night, Sam didn't come home. Neither did his friends. Some of them finally made it home on Wednesday, but three of them never made it out. Two were dead, but they said Sam had been taken prisoner and they couldn't figure out how to rescue him. Then they went back the next day with more men, but Sam had been moved. They couldn't find him. Or find any trace of where he's been taken. I know he's still alive, but I don't know for how much longer."

Beth sobbed.

Sarah moved the mug of tea in front of Beth, who wiped her face again and sipped at the tea. "I can't live without him. We have three kids and this one is coming soon," she said, her hand on her belly. "I can't do it all by myself. I need him. My family's all gone, dead, and his people live back East. There's no one to help take care of the kids. The neighbors have been so kind, but I just need Sam back. And I love him." Beth sobbed again, a deep sound almost like choking.

Cady felt the depth of the pain the woman was in. She closed her eyes, then opened them and nodded.

"What is it you want from me?" Cady asked.

"I need you to find him," said Beth.

"Where did he go?"

"Into the Zoo."

The Zoo had once been a place where animals were caged for peoples' amusement and education. With climate change and changing values, the Zoo had been emptied of animals. A cargo airstrip for small planes and warehouses were built there after the quake. Now, it was a dodgy district where no one entered who didn't have business there. It was completely fenced. The businesses there were run mostly by two different gangs, who still battled for supremacy.

No one in the village knew that Cady had spent years in the Zoo. Back when there were more than the two gangs.

"Whyever did they go there?"

"They had a deal with Roosevelt. To buy some alcohol to sell on this side of the water. Went to pick it up."

Cady shook her head. She didn't know whether the men were dreamers or just idiots. No one on the islands had that kind of money. Most people on this side of the Salish Sound made their own alcohol. But that wasn't the end of Beth's story she knew.

"And? ..." Cady asked.

"Someone ambushed them. It was a trap."

"Who ambushed them?"

"It might have been Roosevelt's people, might have been Morrigu's," said Beth. She picked up the mug with both hand and sipped her tea. An action more to be doing something rather than a need to drink tea. Her hands shook slightly.

"What would Roosevelt gain by that? I don't understand," said Cady.

"He gets the upper hand in the negotiations. He gets complete power over everything as long as he holds Sam hostage. He can demand we pay money for Sam alone. Then want more money for the alcohol."

Cady said, "And Morrigu would get to screw up Roosevelt's dealings."

Beth nodded.

"I don't care who has him, I just want him back," said Beth.

Cady leaned back in her chair, feeling the hard wood grind against her sore shoulders. What Beth wanted was possible, but dangerous.

Cady had spent a lot of time in the Zoo. She'd practically grown up there. She'd run away to the Zoo when she was fifteen, following some boy in. Whose name she soon forgot in her struggle to survive. She'd learned how to steal and fight in one of the smaller gangs who used to run there. Luckily, she hadn't been on either side of the main conflict and had been able to get out. Had survived. Because those who fought for Roosevelt or Morrigu only left the Zoo one way. Dead.

Roosevelt was a 6'5" black human, rumored to have some Blackfoot blood in him. No one knew. He did have powerful magic and was rumored to be ridden by Kalfu, even though Kalfu himself was never seen in this part of the world. He probably preferred warmer climes, lush with heat.

Morrigu was a delicate looking Celtic Goddess. Morrigan, was her full name. Some said she was a mother goddess, or one third of a triple goddess. Others claimed she was a war goddess. Either way, she was a strong being who'd mastered modern technology, such as it was.

Technology hadn't advanced much in the wake of the oceans drowning the land, massive quakes, the flu pandemic and political upheaval. Magic had come flooding back from wherever it had hidden for millennia. So had all the deities of every mythology the planet had ever hosted.

Deities appeared wherever they had followers. Multiple versions of many spirits had seemingly winked into existence. Some diminished, some at full power. Their abilities seemed to wax and wane depending on the strength of their followers' belief. Many moved into the modern world as if they'd never disappeared.

Morrigu had created an entire army. Although human, Roosevelt did too. Their conflict had been going on since before Cady was born and she didn't see any end to it soon, although she hadn't paid attention to goings-on in the Zoo since leaving.

She rubbed her eyes. Both Beth and Sarah were watching her.

Cady asked, "I don't know if I can help you. I haven't been in the Zoo for thirty years. I'm sure things have changed, but I can't fight either Roosevelt or Morrigu."

"We just need you to find him," said Sarah. "Sam's friends will have to get him out."

"As if finding him's an easy thing."

It was and it wasn't. She could find him easily enough, but not getting caught and getting back out was completely different.

She should say no. But then she looked at Beth again. The world was only going to get better if better people were born. If the only humans procreating were the likes of Roosevelt's and Morrigu's followers, the future looked dark indeed.

The least she could do was an exploratory search. See if he was alive and findable, if she went back inside the Zoo, with his friends.

"Do you have anything of your husband's? Something small that's important to him, that I can use to track him?"

Beth pulled a ring out of her pocket.

"He loved this ring, it's been in his family for generations. He hasn't worn it for a while." The woman hesitantly handed it over.

Cady took it. The ring was gold with a red stone in the center, maybe a garnet, and said, *University of Washington, Criminal Justice.* It was heavy, a man's ring. It carried enough of a connection, a tug that could be felt as she rolled it around between her palms. She set it on the table.

Standing, Cady set a candle in the center of the table, lighting it with wooden matches. She could explore at least. See if it was possible to find him easily.

To be of any use though, she'd have to physically go inside the Zoo. That would come later, if her initial exploration worked. Some people or things she just couldn't find. Her magic wouldn't work with them.

She paced around the tiny cabin, centering herself. Silently calling any spirits or allies who could help her, but especially Brigid. Her connection to the deities and other beings from the U.K., or what was left of it, were stronger than any other. Her ancestors came from that part of the world. One of the people who'd taken her in as a child had the full range of genetic tests done. Hoping to identify any disease patterns, but also to give Cady a sense of who her real family was, since she'd lost them all.

She continued to pace, breathing deeply. Monster appeared out from under the bed. Eyeing the strangers warily with his golden eyes, but drawn by the energy Cady was pulling in. He jumped up onto a window sill and began bathing his long, dark fur.

As her spirits came into her consciousness, one by one, a massive black dragon appeared to her volunteering its service. She'd never met a dragon before. This would be interesting.

Cady sat down on the hard wooden chair and picked up the ring, rubbing it between her palms, taking a breath and letting it out slowly. Her roots sank deep into the soil beneath her home, calling up the earth's magic. Drawing it all in until she was filled with energy. She felt the familiar sense of disconnection as her soul left her body. Traveling.

She ran towards the dragon. Her soul and all the helping spirits climbed onto the dragon, who raced down a road, then took flight. They flew fast, quicker than her soul alone could fly.

Soon they were soaring, looking down at the Zoo. Going lower, seeing the flat rooftops of the metal warehouses between the tall maples and firs. Large vehicles were being loaded and unloaded.

Some of the original brick buildings of the former zoo were still standing. Probably still used for offices for the companies who imported goods into the Zoo. Those buildings, and their employees, had been like ambassadors.

No one had touched them. No one was foolish enough to jeopardize the Zoo's lifeline.

Alcohol, drugs, jewelry, art, gas and oil were flown in and stocked here. Until trucks took a ferry over to the Eastside of the water.

Where the truly wealthy, and their armies, lived. Like the

royalty of old. Their servants were like peasants, stuck in those roles for generations. Afraid to leave and go out into an uncertain world.

Not many people drove over to the Eastside. Few roads still ran around the north end of the Salish Sound and all the way to the Eastside. Those that did were blockaded by gangs who charged drivers a heavy toll. Thirty years ago, it was rumored to be at least half the cargo a driver was carrying.

Cady let the tendrils of her consciousness move outward, searching for Sam.

The cargo airport ran along the west side of the Zoo. The rest of the land was warehouses. From there things were trucked down to the boats in Ballard Bay and shipped to the Eastside. Some cargo was flown over in small planes, or put on railcars that took the long way around Salish Sound. The railcars' track were regularly destroyed and the trains looted by individuals or gangs. The rich people on the Eastside rebuilt the tracks. Often their armies accompanied the trains.

The dragon flew lower still, through the remaining trees. Merely a shadow to those with magic to see. The spirits and Cady held invisible against its huge bulk.

She felt the presence of Morrigu and Roosevelt, like beacons. There was a pulse. There, that was Sam. In one of the warehouses. Cady tried to find which one and who it belonged to.

Then the dragon sliced sideways through the air and dove. He curved sharply upwards and away towards Puget Sound. A blood red streak followed them. The dragon wove in and out of the tops of the trees. Attempting to hide.

The red streak followed, taking shape as a demonic being with bat wings. Its humanoid body flew with a speed that matched the dragon's.

"Vanish," she screamed, and found herself back in her body. Heart pounding. Sweat pouring down her forehead. A scuffling noise beneath her bed told her Monster had retreated again.

She opened her eyes and took several deep breaths. Cady set the ring on the table. Then took a sip of her now cold tea, not tasting anything, but grateful for the liquid and the grounding nature of swallowing.

Then she put both her palms flat on the table and let the energy drain away.

She looked at the two women, who watched her intently.

"Your husband is in the Zoo. I couldn't see which warehouse he was in before I was attacked. I don't know who's holding him."

Beth sank down into herself as if completely defeated.

Sarah asked, "Isn't there something else we can do? We really need information."

"Even if I had been able to find him, I still would need to go in with the men. They might move him again. They might have used a decoy to trick anyone searching for him. I can be fooled. Roosevelt's and Morrigu's magics are both powerful and deep."

A thought was coming to her, niggling at her consciousness, but it was lost, when Beth asked, "When can you go?"

"When will the others be ready?"

"Tonight," said Beth.

"I can be ready tonight," she said.

After the two women left, Cady sat down again and drank the rest of her tea.

This was not how she'd planned her day. But finding was one of the few skills she could offer the community, that no one else could do. She took so much it was only fair she gave back when called on. She just hoped that in her next life her soul would choose a skill that wasn't so perilous.

Instead of planting, Cady pulled the wooden box out from under her bed. Monster came out too. Staring warily at her.

In the box were the two guns she'd brought with her from the Zoo. An ancient rifle with a scope and a Glock. She rarely used them these days. Finding lost children generally didn't require a gun.

She cleaned her guns. Monster helped. Then she walked down the muddy road to Tessa's to barter for more ammunition. Taking with her two of the more useless garden books, one of them all about irrigation, now only a curiosity.

When she returned, Cady sharpened her two knives, the big one for on her hip, the other, a stiletto, went in a sheath in her boot. Cady pulled out her essence of death potion, and as an afterthought, pocketed fist-size chunks of labradorite and obsidian. For protection and remaining hidden. She tucked a filled water bottle in her pack, and some dried goat meat. Monster sat watching her, curious about everything.

She had time for a three hour nap and took it. Who knew when she'd get to sleep again?

When she got up, Cady dressed in black pants, a long-sleeved black shirt and black jacket. She pulled on wool socks and laced up her black leather boots with the stiletto in the right one. The boots still had a warped spot where it fit. She hadn't worn these clothes for a couple of decades, but they still fit. A bit musty though, even after airing out on the clothesline all day.

She fixed a goat cheese sandwich from bread she'd made, Joe's tangy goat cheese and some greens from the garden.

She left a note on her table for Joe, telling him when she'd return. Monster would take care of himself. He dined outside, mostly on voles, mice and rats, but he caught the occasional mole or rabbit. Rarely birds. He was a ground cat. He went under when afraid. Never up. She did refill his water bowl.

After dinner, she took her seeds out and planted another section of greens. For the future. The rest she'd have to do when she returned.

Then Cady strapped on the handgun and hip knife, put her small waist pack on. She slung the rifle harness over her head and right shoulder, letting the rifle hang down her back and went to the center of the village to meet up with the others.

2

DAMON

DAMON STOOD AT MORRIGU'S SIDE IN HER THRONE ROOM. A bodyguard to his left and Morrigu's right. The massive warehouse she'd confiscated years ago, which had been dubbed Morrigu's Castle. And indeed, it was a castle. The thick concrete walls lined with rich fabrics in the colors of crimson, black and gold. On top of the fabric hung more stolen paintings than most of the world's remaining museums. Covered with thick bulletproof glass.

At one end sat her golden throne, shimmering in the dim light. They stood in the center of the room. That didn't bode well. She always held audience there when she didn't want to get anything important spattered with blood.

He was getting too old for this job. Yet she wouldn't let him go. Not as long as he was still doing it well. And when he couldn't any longer? Damon figured she'd just kill him. A quick death as a reward for decades of service. It wasn't easy serving a goddess but it had been a long time since he'd any choice.

She watched the strangers intently. A delegation from

Fine Art and Antiques International. Come to explain why their shipment hadn't arrived. Morrigu had good customers waiting for the painting. Customers who paid a small fortune.

The two men and one woman stood there. They all wore business suits, a uniform mostly unchanged for centuries. Since before the earth tried to destroy humans and all they'd built. The two men wore white shirts, signaling their subordination. One of the men had a twitchy cheek. The silence was getting to him. The other man wasn't making eye contact with anyone. The woman was though. She wore a black shirt along with the black suit. A sign she was high enough up in corporate structure to actually make a decision. Her green hair was cut short.

"I have come to offer our apologies," she said to Morrigu, bowing.

Morrigu said nothing. She too, was dressed in black. A long velvet gown with rows of diamonds highlighting each seam of the flared skirt, beneath which delicate, low-heeled black boots peered out. Her bodice cut low for distraction. Long black hair mostly unbound and left flowing to her waist. A circlet of gold and diamonds wove around her head. Her green eyes wide, staring the woman down.

"We are doing everything we can to recover the painting. Pirates attacked the ship and have not sent us a ransom request. We are still pursuing them."

Morrigu still said nothing.

"Is there a way we can make this easier for your customers?" the woman asked.

"A boat. You put the painting on a boat? It is not my clients who have a problem," said Morrigu with a deep, calm voice. "My clients expected the painting a week ago. I could not deliver the product, because you did not get it to me. That makes me look bad. They are disappointed. I am disappointed. They will tell their friends. Word will get around. That hurts my business and my reputation."

"How can we compensate you and your customers?" asked the woman.

"Return their money *and* get my clients their painting."

Damon inwardly smiled.

The woman's features scrunched up in dismay.

"We cannot return their money and get the painting both. Perhaps there is something else we can do."

"You ask me what you can do and then you refuse. Your words are empty," she turned away from them, as if to speak to Damon. Ignoring the woman.

The woman stepped forward. Morrigu's bodyguards moved forward to meet her. She put up her hands and moved back. The bodyguards didn't retreat.

The woman said, "Please, let me explain. We can get you another painting. We brought one on the plane with us. Your cargo supervisor said he would bring it here. A Monet."

She had Morrigu's full attention and it wasn't good. "My clients detest Monet. They only collect Picasso."

"But you could sell the Monet for much more than the Picasso is worth and recoup your customers' money."

"Ah, more work for me to do because of your incompetency. No. I will take the Picasso. You will give me the Monet as a bonus," said Morrigu. She moved forward. The bodyguards parted and the light in the room dimmed, highlighting Morrigu's aura of power.

Damon pitied the woman. It was a losing battle to argue with a deity. She probably knew that. Probably knew she'd been thrown under the wheels by her superiors. The two men, what were they there for anyway? To add enough bodies to the delegation to make it look important?

He scratched his stubble. He still didn't understand business, after all these years. He did understand Morrigu, at least most of the time. His life depended on it.

She was playing with the woman. Seeing how far she could push the other dominant person in the room.

The woman sighed, her shoulders drooped slightly. Knew she was losing.

"I will need to contact my superiors."

The door opened and a cart wheeled in with a painting propped up on it. Remnants of a shipping box lay on the cart. Damon recognized the warehouse woman who wheeled in the cart. He motioned her to come forward.

As the cart drew near, he recognized the painting from one of the books in Morrigu's library. Sunset in Venice. It was on the small side. About 25" by 36". Glorious yellow-orange and contrasting blue. A beautiful painting. It might even be a real Monet. They'd need to call in Jeffries to be sure.

"I don't know if I can sell this," said Morrigu. "People here will either love it because it represents a city that no longer exists or hate it because it's the world they live in. Right next door to a rotting city that's been consumed by the ocean."

"It's worth a small fortune," said the woman. "One of his best, I think. And very overlooked."

Morrigu turned to Damon.

"Call Jeffries. I want to know if this is genuine."

Damon nodded and walked a short distance away. He spoke into his wristband.

"Jeffries." Then paused until he heard the man respond.

"What?"

"You need to get over to the throne room immediately. Morrigu has a painting for you to authenticate."

"Which one?"

"Monet's Sunset in Venice."

"You're joking."

"Have you ever known me to joke."

"No. Sorry. I love this job though. Be right there."

"It's a matter of some urgency."

"Got it."

Damon returned his attention to Morrigu's side.

The woman was on her phone. Probably trying to get approval for Morrigu's outrageous demand. She must have expected it though.

Morrigu had never been reasonable. None of the deities ever were. At least not that he knew of.

Fine Art should have expected her to make demands. She was a good customer. One of the deities with a very exclusive client base. She knew everyone and what they wanted.

Long gone were the days when she and Roosevelt scrapped for the Zoo. Now it was all appearance. To keep the locals away. And to discourage unwanted visitors.

There was still some animosity between the two. Roosevelt wanted the entire place to himself, as did Morrigu. But after nearly a century of fighting, Roosevelt was growing old. He had his family to protect. Young Roosevelt, who was nearing fifty was in charge now. He had a daughter who was next in line.

Jeffries came in the door, pushing a metal cart of supplies. Damon knew what some of the things were, but not others. There was an electronic tool that allowed Jeffries to see different layers of the canvas. To see how an artist worked different sections with layers of paint. To see what brushstrokes went down first, which ones last. One could see if there were other paintings beneath the previous one. It allowed him to compare other paintings by the same artist.

It all seemed like magic to Damon. Then again, magic was very real in this day and age. He nodded to Jeffries to go ahead and do his work.

Jeffries wheeled his cart up next to the one holding the canvas.

The delegation were conferring via conference call with their superiors.

Morrigu just stood at a distance watching Jeffries.

"What else do we have on for today?" she asked.

"Roosevelt wants a meeting," said Damon

"We have nothing to talk about," she said, then snorted.

"He asked. Again."

"What does he want?"

"He wouldn't tell me."

"What do you think he wants?"

"He sounded anxious. As if it was important. Maybe something has come up."

"Like what?" asked Morrigu, turning her green eyes on him. Not emerald green, more stormy green sea.

"I don't have any intel. We lost our only plant in his organization. Haven't been able to get anyone else in close enough."

She nodded.

"He isn't working with the pirates, is he? Did he steal my painting?"

"I don't think his reach is that far," said Damon.

After a time the delegation came over and the woman said, "Fine Art and Antiques will authorize the transaction."

"Which means they'll recover the Picasso, get it to me, and

include the Monet. For no extra cost," said Morrigu. "Provided the Monet is authentic."

"Yes," said the woman. But she didn't look happy about it.

It took a few more minutes before Jeffries said, "It is an authentic Monet."

"Good," said Morrigu. "You can take it to the vault."

Jeffries wheeled the painting out, leaving his cart behind.

"Pleasure doing business with you," said Morrigu, holding up her right hand.

"The same," said the woman, holding up her right hand in agreement.

"I will have the rest of the payment ready for when the Picasso arrives."

The woman opened her mouth, then shut it. What Morrigu demanded wasn't unreasonable, given that they'd lost the painting.

The three of them bowed and then left the room.

"That went well. Although I won't be happy until that Picasso is in my hands. Who knows if they'll ever find it. Damn pirates."

"What shall I tell Roosevelt?" Damon asked.

"Tell him he can come here. I'm very busy right now. He's welcome to bring one unarmed bodyguard. No one else. And get Santoni here for that meeting."

"Will do," said Damon.

Santoni was Morrigu's sorcerer. He was a magical bodyguard. If Roosevelt could only bring an unarmed bodyguard, then he'd bring his new sorcerer. Damon hadn't met her. Another unknown thing which made his senses feel twitchy.

"Anything else?" asked Damon.

"No. Go ahead and contact him. Let me know what time

the meeting is. I'm going to contact our clients and tell them the painting has been stolen. See what they want to do."

She left the room and Damon returned Roosevelt's assistant's call.

They set up a meeting for 2 p.m.

Roosevelt and Morrigu met about once a year. To renew their peace contract. And make decisions about the Zoo in general. It was usually planned long in advance. This was different. It made Damon twitchy. He let Santoni know about the meeting. And scheduled five extra bodyguards, putting everyone else on alert for the next twenty-four hours.

Damon went on about his day. Checking that everyone was where they were supposed to be and things were getting done. He checked that shipments of jewelry and art were moving. And gasoline. Morrigu and Roosevelt shared the gas and oil business. Roosevelt had the wine, beer and other alcohol concessions, Morrigu moved jewelry and art. Their profits were roughly equal and kept that way, which was why they had yearly meetings. Over the years they had grown to know each other's strengths and weaknesses. Neither of them were liars. On that basis their partnership was formed.

Damon rubbed his eyes. He hadn't slept the night before. Something was wrong. He didn't have a great deal of magic, just enough to sense things. His intuition told him that the Zoo was out of balance. He guessed that Roosevelt could explain why. He hoped so. Not knowing what was wrong felt annoying. Damon liked things to run in an orderly manner. Which they rarely did. Still, he could dream.

He made the rounds again. Checking the two warehouses for shipping. Then checking the kitchen. During which he grabbed three warm cookies which would suffice for lunch. He passed through all the main rooms in Morrigu's "palace", as she called it.

Spring was coming, but the weather felt cold and even the rain had a bite to it. All his old wounds ached. He'd once been Morrigu's bodyguard. Before he'd grown too old. Back then, James had been her advisor. He'd trained Damon to take over the job. Decided Damon had the personality and organizational skills to do the job. Then James died. Cancer.

The damn disease was over a million years old and still there was no cure. And with the intellectual decline of the world, it might be a million more years before scientists came up with one. At least things were moving forward again. Humanity had survived, but the world was still too unstable.

It was time.

Damon went to the entrance to make sure guards were in place. Then checked Morrigu's audience chamber again. Santoni and two other bodyguards were waiting. Morrigu came in and sat on her throne.

She told one of the staff, "Please get us some coffee and pastries."

The young woman left for the kitchen.

Damon returned to the entrance to wait for Roosevelt and make sure things went as planned.

3

EVANGELINE

EVANGELINE FOLLOWED ROOSEVELT THROUGH THE pouring rain to the entrance of Morrigu's warehouse. An extraordinarily large contingent of crows took flight. Diving at them and cawing angrily. She could feel their combined hatred of intruders.

Roosevelt hurried inside the sliding door and she followed him. Evangeline shook off her gold and green embroidered cloak once inside.

Evangeline hated the rain. Hated this part of the country. Where she came from rain gave life, here it just drowned everything. Roosevelt might not be paying her enough to be here. She'd only been in his employment for a few months now.

One of Morrigu's staff took her cloak and Roosevelt's leather jacket. This left her wearing black leggings and a loose gold shirt that shimmered in the dim light. And her black leather boots. Evangeline's long black hair was elaborately braided and the braids tied into one mass, out of her way.

Her gold necklace contained black seeds that would pop

open as incendiary devices. Each one a small bomb. Those might not be necessary either, but were always good to have on hand.

No one searched her, so she dropped the glamour that hid the small pistol beneath her loose shirt. She didn't think she'd need the pistol. The gold shirt glimmered and shifted, all on its own, making a beautiful contrast to her dark black skin. Not blue-black like Roosevelt, but much darker than the white guy who took her cloak. Her whole life, she was always the darkest person in the room. She was used to it and dressed to play that up. Often in white, which always made a great contrast when blood was drawn.

They walked farther inside. Evangeline had to hand it to Morrigu. On the inside the place didn't look like a warehouse. The interior walls of the entryway looked like stonework. The next room had walls hung with rich tapestries with fancy, expensive art. Much of it authentic, Roosevelt had told her, and by old masters.

Why were they always old masters? Where were the paintings by women? Probably unpainted or uncredited. Women always got stomped on in this world. Since history had begun to be written down.

It was time for a change. Pity she had to do it through a man.

At the end of the room, Morrigu and her sorcerer, Santoni, stood by several upholstered chairs arranged in a circle, around a low table. So, the goddess envisioned this as a casual business meeting. Fool. Had she thought Roosevelt wouldn't find out about her spy?

Roosevelt greeted Morrigu, bowing. Evangeline followed his example, out of curtesy.

Morrigu and Roosevelt sat across the table from each

other. Santoni had not taken his eyes off either Roosevelt or herself since they entered the room. He sat in the chair next to Morrigu. Evangeline remained standing. It made her look out of place in the huge, nearly empty room, but today, she was the unarmed bodyguard. She needed to stand.

She felt Santoni attempting to search her and focused her attention on the conversation between Roosevelt and Morrigu. Santoni would get nothing from her that she didn't want to give. From Roosevelt either.

Evangeline knew Santoni was rumored to be powerful. He was tenacious, but unimaginative. She was much stronger. She was a jaguar, standing camouflaged in plain sight. Ready to spring, if necessary.

Roosevelt said, "I hear you are very busy today," in his melodic voice.

Morrigu said, "I am. Meeting after meeting, after meeting. I had problems with an art shipment and the company sent people out to negotiate. That was rather dull. So now I have to go over to the Eastside and meet with my buyers. Offer them something else. They're not going to be happy. And I need to search out a new opal supplier for a customer who's discovered a sudden passion for opals."

Roosevelt said nothing.

"Why did you want to meet?" she asked.

"I want to discuss the terms of our agreement," he said, in a calm voice.

Morrigu looked momentarily shocked, then covered it with a look of concern. "What about them?"

"Things that were once fair and equitable, are no longer."

"What things?"

"There are others who are providing fine alcohol, and drugs, to the Eastside. Their business is growing and mine shrinks. I do not have the power to drive them out. I am using all my resources to deliver our gas and oil where it's needed, there's none left over to fight a war on the Eastside. And the profit from even that is shrinking. People are turning to solar and wind more and more."

"Well, when we began our agreement, we always knew gas and oil were on their way out," said Morrigu.

"It costs too much to deliver now, and to ship in. It is not worth it."

Evangeline frowned. What he wasn't saying was that Morrigu was not out drumming up more sales. That was her part of the agreement. She'd shifted her attention almost completely to selling art and jewels.

"Well, then let's drop it. It'll mean a cut in income though."

"It would allow me to focus on driving my competition out of business. I need to lean on them more."

"Do your competitors have armies?"

"Everyone on the Eastside has armies. I must bulk up my own army. Make a base over there before they can grow larger and stronger."

Two of Morrigu's people brought in a tray with food and drink. Coffee was poured and distributed around the table.

Evangeline didn't take anything. She was working, but she could smell the delicious aroma. The scent of it made her feel warm in the coolness of the warehouse.

Santoni took a mug of coffee. Evangeline inwardly sneered at his bodyguard skills. He was stupid. No matter how much magic he had. Then again, he was protecting Morrigu, a goddess. Roosevelt was not a god. She had innate immortality. Roosevelt just had powerful sorcery and very advanced martial skills.

Morrigu sipped her coffee and set the mug down. She said, "So you want us to shut down the gas and oil business? Freeing you up to strengthen your hold on alcohol?"

"Yes, but more than that. I want us to combine all our business. The profits and the losses. The alcohol side is going to sustain heavy losses over the next few years, as it does when one begins a war. Once the competition's gone, it will become even more profitable."

Morrigu looked shocked.

It was a ballsy move. Asking Morrigu to finance his war and split her profits from selling art and jewels. Evangeline had to admire him for that.

"I don't know," said Morrigu, struggling for words.

"I want us to be full partners, no secrets, complete transparency."

"I don't work that way," said Morrigu. "I can't. I need to have full power to negotiate what I need to, without worrying that someone else won't like what I've done."

Evangeline tried to work through what Roosevelt's game was. He always seemed to have one going. Had he and Morrigu been lovers once? He was making a request that would have gotten him killed in most business circumstances she'd witnessed.

Roosevelt said, "You would, of course, have full negotiation power. Negotiation is one of your gifts. I've watched you work."

If that was the case, why wasn't the goddess turning him down outright? Evangeline knew there must be a relationship beneath the surface that she wasn't seeing, but couldn't sense what it was. Had Roosevelt saved Morrigu's ass once upon a time? Did she owe him?

A man who looked to be in his late forties, early fifties,

entered the room. His brown-gray hair had a buzz cut and he moved like one who kept in shape, but felt the ache of old injuries. Still, there was a presence about him that made her wary. He didn't have much magic, or perhaps kept it under wraps, but she sensed an enormous amount of power. She didn't want to tangle with him.

He came to the circle and bowed.

"Excuse me," he said.

"What is it Damon?" Morrigu asked.

Then he bent over and whispered something in Morrigu's ear.

The goddess' eyes widened and her mouth dropped open.

"Those bastards," she said, clenching her hands. "How dare they?"

The man straightened, waiting.

She said to Roosevelt, "The art world too has its interlopers. This morning I was told that a Picasso I was expecting for a client had been stolen. Now I have found out the painting was stolen by one of my own competitors. I don't know if they're planning on selling it to my client or someone else. This is outrageous. I shall destroy them."

Evangeline watched as the aura of the goddess blazed red-orange. Morrigu rose from the chair and began pacing behind it like a caged jaguar. Roosevelt glanced up at Evangeline and she shook her head slightly as if to say, *whatever it is you want to do, don't. Leave her alone.*

The goddess was one of the most dangerous beings she'd ever met. Evangeline hadn't often seen that level of rage, but it was always deadly. And the goddess' control was what frightened her most. That sort of control meant the ability to be deadly accurate when she did kill.

Evangeline noticed Damon studying her. Gauging her power.

When Morrigu was the deadly one in the room.

Evangeline had the feeling he could see right through her. He also hid the amount of power he held. Not giving anything away. The unknown was so much harder to deal with. Evangeline hated working with people like that. There was no way to gauge the enemy's strength. And he probably was her enemy. Until Roosevelt told her otherwise. He might not be Morrigu's sorcerer, but he was powerful.

Even though Evangeline could see his old injuries, she had a feeling he could beat her to a pulp. Despite all her training. She was younger and more flexible. He was older and probably more skilled. He carried a sense of strong physical power, more than someone his size should.

Roosevelt drank more coffee and ate some of the sweet bread on the table, as did Morrigu's sorcerer. Damon stood on the other side of the furniture, waiting for Morrigu's instructions.

Evangeline just watched the scene.

Morrigu still paced. Then she'd stop and stare into space. Then move again. Finally, she stopped behind her chair.

"I don't know how to get to my enemies," she said. "They are beyond my reach."

"What will you do?" asked Roosevelt.

"I must travel. Go to them."

"Where are they?" he asked.

"New London."

Evangeline straightened in surprise.

Decades ago, London had been moved. The entire population of the city had moved farther inland, government and many historic buildings, rebuilt from the original stones.

Piece by piece. There had been too many quakes and flooding in old London. The entire city had become dysfunctional. And the pandemic had cut the population in half.

Morrigu must really want revenge, to travel to the other side of the world.

"Will you lose power if you go there? So close to your old home?"

Evangeline hadn't considered that. What happened to deities present in the new world, if they returned to the old world where surely the same deity manifested? Were they at war with each other? Did they merge and become one being? Or was their power doubled somehow?

"I don't know," said Morrigu. "I don't know if any of my people are in New London."

Evangeline's body began to ache from standing in the same position. She moved ever so slightly. Just enough to keep her muscles alert and ready for action.

She could smell the coffee and longed for a cup, but she was working. Morrigu's man still watched her. Taking her measure. Santoni didn't. He was a smug, self-centered bastard with an ego the size of the planet. Which meant he'd fall soon. Morrigu should have chosen better.

Roosevelt said, "Can you lure your enemies here?"

Morrigu turned and stared at him.

"I don't know them well enough. I don't know what I could use to draw them across the world."

"And yet, you're allowing yourself to be drawn there. By strangers."

"You're right. I can't go there. It's too dangerous to go so close to where I'm from. There's sure to be another Morrigu. A stronger one, perhaps. I don't know what would happen."

"Let us lay a trap for them then," said Roosevelt.

"How?" asked Morrigu.

"Find out what they want. Send someone there and infiltrate the business."

"I can do that. I have just the person," she said. She turned to Damon. "Jeffries. He'd be perfect."

Damon raised an eyebrow.

"What?" she asked.

"He doesn't know anything about anything other than art. He'd make a terrible spy," Damon said.

"Exactly. No one will suspect him. But he will be able to get inside with his skill," said Morrigu.

Damon cocked his head in acknowledgment.

"Good. We will send him and then begin to plan their downfall."

Damon nodded.

"Go tell him to begin packing," said Morrigu.

Damon bowed and left the room.

Evangeline felt a sense of relief. One less person to keep track of. One less body she might need to fight.

Roosevelt said, "So, do we have an agreement? We will stop selling gas and oil. You and I will combine our other ventures, alcohol, drugs, art and jewels into one business. And support each other. No secrets."

Morrigu sat down in her chair again and stared at him.

"We will need to talk further about all this. I don't understand your business at all and I'm guessing there's things about my business you will need to learn."

"I agree. Shall we take four mornings each week to learn about each other's business?" he asked.

"I think that would be a good start."

"Good, let us shake on it," he said, standing and holding out his hand.

Morrigu stood and took his hand, shaking it.

"I do have a thorny problem I need help with," said Roosevelt.

"What?"

"Last week a group of locals, at least that's what they said they were, asked for a meeting to buy alcohol for this side. Then they came two days ago, sneaking in like thieves. My people thought they were. We're not used to dealing with locals. All but one got away. We have him, he was wounded, so we gave him medical care. It turns out he has the sight. Not short-term sight, but long-range sight. He told me you and I would form a cartel that would cover the world."

"So what is your problem?" she asked.

"I don't want to let him go."

"So don't."

Evangeline listened with interest. So that was Roosevelt's strategy. To use the man as a tool to get Morrigu further invested in his business. A plea for help. To ask her for help, instead of accusing her of spying on him. It was still not clear to Evangeline if the man with the sight was a spy or not. Or if Roosevelt had caught someone else who was the actual spy. He hadn't confided in her.

"They will keep coming for him."

"Can you not convince him to work for you?" asked Morrigu.

"Not so far. He wants to go home. His wife or kids or something like that."

"And he cannot live there and still work for you?"

"It's not convenient."

"But surely if his gift of sight is only long-range you would not need him very often. You could send for him," said Morrigu.

"I don't know. I don't trust the locals. I don't trust that he'd come back."

"If you kill his friends when they come back for him, he certainly won't return and help you."

"What would you do?" asked Roosevelt.

"Well, I could be more helpful if I talked to him. Perhaps I can find some leverage that you can't. Many of these locals have run in the Zoo, when they were younger. When our dead competitors had business here. When the two of us were at war."

"That's a good idea. Shall we go now?" Roosevelt asked.

"Damon will come with us. He recognizes everyone. And Santoni."

"Of course," said Roosevelt.

Evangeline took a deep breath. Oh good. A field trip with our enemy.

Morrigu said, "The three of us will take my car. Where should we meet you?"

"Warehouse 27," said Roosevelt. "I'll go and alert my guards that you'll be following us."

Roosevelt stood, bowed and moved towards the entrance. Evangeline followed, still wary.

They got their coats without incident and went back out into the rain.

Once inside the big black sedan, Roosevelt grinned and said, "That went well."

Evangeline rolled her eyes at him.

"What? I got her to split the businesses, her lucrative ones and my not so lucrative ones. I got her to dump the gas and oil. And I've got my war coming up, with finances for it. I'd say that was a good day's work."

"It is, it certainly is," said Evangeline.

"But?"

"Can you trust her?"

"No, of course not. 'Keep your friends close and your enemies closer.'"

"Well, you certainly got her closer."

He leaned back against the seat, his grin growing ever wider.

The car moved slowly down the darkening road to the warehouse.

4

CADY

By the time Cady got to the center of the village, most of the others were waiting. Five men, four women. All dressed in black and carrying weapons. Some of them wore body armor on the outside of their clothes. Cady guessed she probably should have, but didn't have any. She'd left the Zoo when most of the fighting was knives and handguns. Not machine guns.

She knew some of them. Joaquin raised sheep and llamas. His family spun wool and made clothes for the village. Ryan helped people build and repair houses. Gia was the villages' librarian. She did research and found information for people. Only the rich had access to the internet, provided it still existed. No one in the village was rich. Sharine was a doctor and veterinarian. One of two in the village. Will was a genius with machinery.

The person in charge was Mazzy. She was a tall Asian woman with short hair. A formidable take charge sort of person, who often organized village events. That Cady never went to.

"This is what we're going to do," she said. "We'll enter on the other side of the Zoo. The west side, where the runway is. Last time we went in on the east. No doubt they've discovered and closed that hole. We'll wait until a plane lands and there are bodies running around doing their jobs. That's our distraction. We'll pass through the Zoo, over to the warehouses. They've still got strips of trees and shrubs there, we'll travel near those. Then Cady will lead us to where they're holding Sam. Questions?"

"I have one," asked Cady. "Why are they holding Joe? What's so special about him?"

Most people shrugged. Sarah and Beth were there. Cady stared at Sarah. Sarah said nothing, but she looked uncomfortable.

"If we don't know why, it's only going to cause us more trouble, perhaps get us killed," said Mazzy.

Sarah gave a deep sigh, her hand on her belly.

Then she said, "Sam has the sight. Not like what will happen tomorrow. More like what will happen decades from now. If they've discovered that, and they might have, they'll want to keep him. That's why we don't talk about it. We've told no one here in the village, I'm sorry."

"Well, I suspect you're right," said Cady. "He'd be a useful tool to either Roosevelt or Morrigu."

"Do you think Morrigu's involved?" asked Mazzy.

"I don't know. It's unclear who has him. I was attacked when I tried to find out. He's in one of the northern warehouses. I didn't have time to find the exact one. And I don't know which warehouses are Roosevelt's or Morrigu's any more," said Cady.

"Okay, we'll be moving on the fly here," said Mazzy. "We've got earbuds. I expect you to use them and not turn them off once we enter the Zoo." She handed a pair to Cady, who inserted them in her ear and tested them.

Mazzy continued, "Joaquin is the only one of us who can do an invisibility spell. Stay close to him."

"I am not very good at it," Joaquin said. "It will not be complete and I can't keep it up for long. It's the best I have to offer."

"Better than the rest of us can do," said Will.

The others hugged their loved ones. Cady had no one to say goodbye to. She never had.

She was the first one in the electric van. They drove out of the village, on the one good road. Many of the roads had buckled during the quake decades past. The main road had been repaired, most of the others hadn't. The grid that had once been Seattle, no longer functioned. They drove past houses and business that were sunken with year upon year of rain damage. Or had been scavenged, windows gone, doors taken. Wood peeled off. Entire blocks in ruins.

Nature had taken much of it back. First had come bindweed and blackberries. Then trees grew up through and around the ruins. Big leaf maples and Douglas firs over thirty meters tall. The native trees dominated, although there were plenty of smaller trees of all types too.

Every now and then, they drove past a small village or a single dwelling which had been rebuilt and people who had livestock. One never went to close to those loners. It was a good way to end up dead. They generally protected their livestock with dogs and guns.

It took about half an hour to get to the Zoo. The driver, Jeanne, let them off and went to drive over to the northwest corner of the Zoo. There was more cover from the trees for her to park and wait for them to come out. The warehouses were closer to the fence there. They might need to carry Sam out. One of the men, Will who topped 6'6", carried a collapsible stretcher in his backpack. Mazzy had thought of everything.

It was full dark now, although there was a waning moon tonight. Cady pulled on her leather gloves as she walked towards the fence. She felt on edge, wired. The air smelled fresh, a breeze coming off the Sound. Not much smoke, the days and evenings warming as spring came. They were all squatting down, next to the fence, turning their earbuds on.

Ryan had bolt cutters and was working on the wire fence. Lights lined the short runway, making it easy for the planes to land. Three planes and a helicopter were parked down at this end, tethered to metal loops embedded in the asphalt. The wind here got fierce sometimes. Too many trees had been taken down and winter storms whipped through.

Once Ryan had cut an opening, he put the bolt cutters in his pack. They all slithered through the hole and he pulled it closed again, to disguise it. Then they moved along the fence in the shadows, keeping low. Squatting or crawling. It was slow going.

A plane landed on the runway and its light blasted the fence area. They all lay flat. Cady's heart pounding louder than the plane's engines. It taxied down the runway, turning and they were in darkness again. They moved faster.

As the plane stopped, people came running out and unloaded it. Now they were able to move more quickly. The first row of trees and shrubs was up ahead. Just a small patch of open ground to cover. They clumped around Joaquin, covered by his spell, at least temporarily.

They slunk along the shrubs until they got to the warehouses. Now it was Cady's turn. They hid inside a large clump of trees and rhodies, covered by the evergreen foliage.

Invisible from the road inside the Zoo and from the fence. They heard a couple of guards patrolling along the fence. Cady hoped the opening in the fence was disguised enough. Maybe the guards would be drunk or distracted by the new shipment of whatever the plane was carrying.

Cady got everyone's attention and then sat down on the damp soil. The others circled around her in amongst the wet shrubbery. She closed her eyes and grounded herself, feeling energy coming up from the earth and down from the sky. She mingled those two energies together, mixing the dark and the light. She called a circle of protection around them and felt the boundary firm up with energy from Gia and Will. They concealed her magic.

Which was a good thing. She could sense the same demons she'd met when coming to the Zoo in her journey with the dragon. They swirled around the warehouses, seeking intruders. By some miracle, they hadn't felt the villagers' presence yet. Cady pulled more energy from Gia and Will.

Then she called all the guides who'd been with her earlier in the day. Including the dragon. Their spirits ventured out into the road and past all the warehouses. Searching for Sam. The first warehouse was empty of people. Same with the second. The third warehouse had two men in it, neither of them Sam.

The fourth warehouse. That's where he was. Cady felt one other person in the warehouse. She couldn't tell if it was a guard, or if they were awake or asleep. But Sam was alive. She scouted around the next two warehouses and found them empty.

Then she returned to her body. Grounded herself and opened her eyes. She spoke softly into the com, relaying the information.

Mazzy spoke into the com. "Okay, we'll go in through the front. Cluster around Joaquin until we get inside. Ryan will get us in the door if it's locked. Sharine, Mateo, Will and I will go in first and take out the guard, we have suppressors for our rifles. The rest of you take cover, inside and near the door if possible, until I tell you to move. No sense all of us getting shot up."

They moved across the road and past the first three warehouses, covered by Joaquin's spell. Their weapons were all out. Cady's rifle felt solid in her hand. It had been a long time since she used it. Even longer since she used it on a person.

She could feel her energy amped up. Ready to fight. Aware of everyone around her. The rain misted down through the near darkness. Behind the clouds, the moon shone, but not enough to break through and spread actual light on the earth. There were lights on the warehouses and on the road. The one nearest the fourth warehouse was burnt out. Things hadn't been so well-lit last time she was in the Zoo. Lights got shot out back in the day.

Ryan was working the lock, then Cady heard the door open and everyone began moving inside. They walked into the darkness and away from the light the door let in. Someone closed the door. Cady moved slowly to stand against the wall. She assumed the others did the same. She could see nothing. The air felt heavy. There was no noise, so nobody ran into anything. The room smelled of wine.

Mazzy lit a dim light and shone it around quickly, before putting it out. They were in a small room, an entryway. There was a partition between this room and the main warehouse. Mazzy, Sharine, Will and Mateo headed towards the door to the main warehouse. The others stood along the wall, like

Cady. Trying to stay silent. There was nowhere to hide. It was a nearly empty room. One table covered with paperwork, clipboards. A row of hooks to hang coats on. A door that went off to the left. Will opened that. It led to stairs. He went up alone. Surprisingly silent for such a big man.

The door to the warehouse opened and closed. No light came in, so the warehouse was being kept dark. The smell of wine was stronger there. Bottles always got broken and spilled. The smell lingered. It smelled like a winery. Her neighbor Tank had a small building near his house, it had once been a garage for housing cars. He turned it into a winery and kept barrels of various wines, ciders and mead. It smelled like this one.

Waiting felt eternal. Cady breathed deeply. Keeping alert. She went deep inside herself and let her guides feel around. Joe was in the main warehouse. The guard upstairs.

She spoke softly into the com. "The guard's upstairs."

Cady turned a small flashlight on and pointed to the open door and stairs that Will had gone up. Gia and Ryan moved towards the door, opened it and went slowly up.

Cady switched the light off.

There was scuffling above them. Then the sound of a handgun with a silencer. Several shots. Cady couldn't differentiate between any of the people above.

All they could do was wait longer.

All of a sudden lights came on in the room they were standing in. Then Will, Gia and Ryan came down the stairs, quickly and loudly. They turned and ran towards the main room of the warehouse.

Cady and the other followed. The entire warehouse was fully lit now. The room was filled with pallets of boxes, stacked about two and half meters high. Presumably filled with wine and other alcohol. Cady could see the upper level had glass windows to look down upon the floor.

There was a room off the warehouse and beneath the upper room. The door was open to it, but the room was dark. Probably a break room or an office.

She followed Will and the others to the back corner. There were huge doors that probably opened onto a loading dock. On a chair sat a man, bent over and bloody, barely conscious. Sam. Ryan was on his knees, cutting the zip ties that held Sam still. Sharine was digging in her pack for meds.

As soon as Will got there, he asked, "Stretcher?"

Mazzy said, "Yes."

Will pulled it out of his pack and began pulling out the rods, turning them so they were solid. By the time Ryan had Sam cut loose, Will had the stretcher together.

Sharine gave Sam a shot of something and said, "That's the best I can do, until I have time to examine him. His cuts and bruises will take some time to care for and I don't know what else might be wrong."

Will, Tank and Joaquin lifted Sam onto the stretcher. After Sam was strapped in, Will and Tank lifted the stretcher.

Mazzy said, "Let's get out of here."

They were moving back towards the door where they came in from when they heard voices from that direction.

Mazzy said on the com, "We've got company."

"There's a room over there," said Cady, pointing.

They headed that way and made it just in time, closing the door. There was a small window to the warehouse. Cady peered out it.

She saw Roosevelt, a flashily dressed black woman all in gold, and six bodyguards enter and walk towards the back of the warehouse, disappearing behind the pallets of wine.

Mazzy stood next to her, looking out the window.

Mazzy said, "On the count of three, run for the front."

They were almost ready to make a run for it when Cady felt a surge of power.

"No wait," Cady said.

Three more guards walked in through the front. Followed by a slight man who walked as if he had all the power in the world. Which he didn't, Cady sensed. Then came Morrigu. Ah, there was the source of the power surge. Morrigu. Followed by eight more guards. They all walked to the back, where the yelling was coming from. Two of Roosevelt's guards, running towards the front, met them.

There was no way out now.

Cady looked at Mazzy. Who looked at her.

"Shit," said Mazzy. "Run, fight or hide?"

Cady shone her small flashlight around. The room they were in was small. Only a fake wood table, some ancient plastic chairs and a refrigerator. Nowhere to hide. She switched it off.

There was no hiding out in the main warehouse. It was all straight rows and the pallets were placed to close together.

She heard footsteps above them and more yelling.

The dragon came into her mind and howled, "Run! Fight! Go!"

"Run and fight," said Cady. "Nowhere to hide. They'll check here soon."

"Ryan, as soon and you can, make a break for it and make sure that hole in the fence is open. Those of us with guns, give Will and Tank some cover. They'll need to move slower with the stretcher."

Cady pulled out her handgun and held it in her left hand. She wasn't quite as accurate with it, but better two guns than one. They opened the door and ran out of the room and around the corner to the front entrance. Mateo and Sharine first. They were able to take out the two guards coming back down the stairs.

They kept running. Ryan sprinted for the fence line. Followed by Will and Tank. Mateo and Sharine, the best shots, let others pass them and moved to the rear. Guards flowed out the building, followed by the slight man without much power.

He stood apart, trying to gather his power.

Mazzy stood near Cady and she raised one hand and zapped him with a spell of something that made him fall to his knees. Cady hadn't known Mazzy had that much magic.

They ran again. The guards followed and so did the black woman in gold. She swirled her arms and down came a heavy golden net, over them. It twined around them, inhibiting all large movement.

Cady kept shooting and went for the stiletto in her boot, but never made it. As the net dropped over them, the black woman said something Cady didn't understand and she felt herself lose consciousness.

5

DAMON

DAMON, MORRIGU AND HER GUARDS STOOD ON ALERT outside Roosevelt's warehouse. Santoni had fled when the gunfire started. Little bastard.

The scuffle they'd arrived in the middle of had put everyone's back up. Damon felt twitchy. He wanted to make someone pay for putting Morrigu in the middle of this. There was no way for him to do that. It had been Roosevelt's incompetence. And Morrigu was bringing herself ever closer to the man. For reasons Damon couldn't understand.

It was about some larger plan she had and wasn't sharing with him. Some plan for world domination. Or at least this small world.

He breathed deeply, trying to maintain control of himself and let out all the excess energy. The other guards were doing the same. Taking their cues from him. Morrigu was studying the scene. Plotting and planning, as she often did. He didn't understand the goddess at all.

In the middle of the road lay several people seemingly asleep, covered with a gold net. Roosevelt and the sorceress were talking. His guards reaching through the net, taking the prisoners' weapons.

One of Roosevelt's advisors, Jack, explained to Morrigu what was happening.

"These people are local villagers, trying to rescue the man who Roosevelt caught and was holding. That man has now escaped, along with a few other villagers, but Roosevelt's sorcerer has caught about half of the villagers. They are mostly unharmed."

Roosevelt was furious, his face puffing up like it was about to blow. He was giving his head of security a dressing down. Not just for the escapees, but also for the second intrusion in a week. The guy stood with his head down, knowing he'd screwed up royally.

Damon would have handled that in private. It wasn't good to show your weaknesses to others.

Roosevelt's sorcerer was amazing. To catch so many and not harm a one. Roosevelt's goons had managed to wound one of them, but that's all the damage they'd been able to do.

Santoni should have been helping guard Morrigu. She needed to replace him. Damon wanted to fire his ass. And then kill him. But he didn't have the power to do it.

Only Morrigu did. Damon hoped she'd get rid of him sooner rather than later. He suspected she kept Santoni around because he wasn't strong enough to threaten her power. Damon wasn't sure if it would be wise to remind her that wasn't a good strategy. He'd do it anyway.

Roosevelt's sorcerer removed the net from the prisoners and Morrigu's guards dragged them to one of Morrigu's warehouses. One with cells below ground, one for each of the prisoners.

Damon organized the guard duty and called the doctor to

see to the prisoner's gunshot wound. He arranged for food and water.

Damon stood inside one of the interrogation rooms. Waiting for Morrigu and Roosevelt. And whoever Roosevelt decided to bring. Probably, his sorcerer.

The room was a pasty green color which annoyed him. It was supposed to be calming, so the suspect or victim would talk. That wouldn't have worked for him.

The place smelled too clean. The lights shone too bright. He wanted out of here. The dungeon, as Morrigu called it, always made him feel trapped. There was only one way in and out. If they were attacked down here, there was no quick escape. And the situation was even more irritating.

There was really no sense to any of this. They should just let the people go. They were villagers. The only reason for their presence here was to rescue one of their own. Morrigu had told Damon about Roosevelt's version of the events that led up to this. She said he was being cagey and untruthful. Apparently, the locals had wanted to buy alcohol from him. Roosevelt said they snuck in like thieves. Probably not the case. Roosevelt had just found the seer and wanted to justify keeping him. Chased the others off, not thinking of the consequences.

Damon didn't want to wage a meaningless war with the locals. That would be a pointless, probably un-winnable war. The villagers had something to fight for that was dear to them: family, friends and their homes. Not worth battling them for those.

Morrigu swept into the room, dressed in green velvet pants and tunic. Her feet in green suede boots. A huge rough cut emerald hung from a silver chain around her neck.

She sat in one of the green plastic chairs, flipping her long, dark hair back. The guard following her, handed Morrigu a cup of tea, then left to stand outside the room.

She looked at Damon and gave a heavy sigh.

"I know. This is ridiculous. We'll let him play for awhile and then I'll rein him in."

"If he hurts any of them, the village won't forget it," said Damon.

"You're not afraid, are you?"

"No, but I don't think we should go courting trouble. Especially from those who aren't our enemies. It's one thing to go against your competitors. Another thing to go against his. And it's foolish to create a war with your neighbors where there wasn't one. They've always kept to themselves and left us alone. I think we should toss them out and forget about them."

"I'll keep that in mind, Advisor."

He stiffened inside. Was that an insult, putting him in his place? Or was it a term of endearment? He could never tell with her.

She said, "Santoni has been found at the Castle. You were looking for him, I believe."

Damon nodded.

The Castle was Morrigu's main warehouse. Idiot. the man probably didn't even know he'd done anything wrong.

There were voices in the hallway. Roosevelt. His loud voice boomed through the lower level of the warehouse. Damon stood behind Morrigu, at attention.

Roosevelt's bulk entered the door, making the frame look small. He came in and plunked down in the chair opposite Morrigu. Evangeline followed, taking a place between Roosevelt and the wall. Both of them looked angry.

"Four men wounded," Roosevelt growled. "Those villagers are gonna pay."

"For what?" asked Morrigu. "Rescuing their friend who came to buy alcohol from you? A man who you wanted to keep, but who didn't want to stay? Is this the war you really want to fight?"

"Hell yes."

"What about your plans to go after your competitors? You don't have enough of an army to fight on two fronts."

Roosevelt just stared at her.

Morrigu said, "You know I'm right. I'm a goddess of war. Your people outnumbered the villagers and yet, five or six got away. You caught five with the skill of your sorcerer, not your guards. They shot one and four of them got shot. I don't think they're ready for a fight. Any fight. They've grown soft in the years there's been no war."

Damon watch Roosevelt closely. The man looked ready to blow again. He glanced at Evangeline. She looked alert and ready for anything. He'd only seen her a handful to times, but she always looked that way. Too bad Morrigu hadn't hired her before Roosevelt had. Evangeline was capable.

He felt Morrigu's power reach out to calm Roosevelt.

She said, "Perhaps if you had ten or more sorcerers with the skill of this one, you might be able to dispatch the villagers and move on to your competitors. But to what end? Bothering with the villagers gains you nothing. No power, no resources. They are poor people, living on the edge. Let them be and concentrate on your competitors. Train your army."

Roosevelt softened a bit

"What do we do with them?" he asked. "You're right, of course. I don't have time for a war with them. I need to attack my competitors before they become more entrenched."

"Let them go," said Morrigu. "I'll make sure they get back home. We have war plans to make."

"We?" asked Roosevelt.

"You asked to change our agreement. To share everything. There is the alcohol and drug war. And also the trap to lure my competition out here. We must plan both. And see which one is more effective to fight first."

Damon felt the energy in the room shift. He didn't know if it was Morrigu or Roosevelt. Suddenly there was a relief. A feeling of energy moving forward instead of sideways. Magic swirled through the air. Damon couldn't do magic, but he could sense it. This felt overpowering and easy to notice.

It didn't feel like Morrigu. He wasn't as familiar with Roosevelt's magic. And surely, if it was Evangeline, she would be more subtle. She seemed to be an all or nothing sort of person.

He looked at her and she stood there, staring at the wall. Like a good bodyguard should do when overhearing an intimate conversation.

"Let us plan, then," said Roosevelt.

"Damon, I'd like you personally to see to the release of the prisoners. Take the bus and drive them back home. See they get there safely, and smooth things over. Roosevelt, can we give them a case or two of wine?"

Roosevelt waved his hand. "Give them five. Evangeline, go with him. I want you to make sure the village is not a threat to us."

"Good idea," said Morrigu.

Damon bowed and hoped there wasn't a hidden message in Roosevelt's words.

Evangeline followed him out of the room.

Damon went to the guard center, just outside the cells.

"Gather the prisoners," he said to one of the guards. To the other, "Gather up their belongings and return them. Keep all the weapons separate."

Then Damon spoke into his wristband, calling Eamon, the guard who oversaw transportation. "Get the van, go to Roosevelt's warehouse. "What number is it?" he asked Evangeline.

She said, "Number ten, I'll go arrange the wine and meet the van on the loading dock, before we come back here."

Damon nodded, but she was already gone.

"Go to number 10. Pick up five cases of wine and Roosevelt's sorcerer. Then come to the Dungeon to pick me and the prisoners up."

"Where we going, boss?"

"We're taking them home. Bring a couple of guards who are on the mellow side, but smart and seasoned. Just in case there's trouble. Unarmed guards."

"Will do. See you in ten," said Eamon.

Damon had the guard let him inside the cell complex. The five prisoners stood outside their rooms, each of them in brown jumpsuits. One of them, an older woman, looked ashen. She leaned against the wall. The guard stood at the other end of the hall.

"Get this woman a chair," he said to the guard, who rushed off to find one.

The guard returned quickly with a chair and the older woman sank down into it. Damon knew her. He couldn't place her though. But something was very familiar. Not the long gray hair though.

"I'm Damon and I work for Morrigu. She is not responsible for your capture. Or for your friend, the seer's capture either. However, she has persuaded Roosevelt to let you go. Neither of them wants a war with our neighbors. The guards will take you back to your cells and return your belongings. Once you've changed, we will take you home."

A tall woman, maybe part Japanese, asked, "That makes no sense."

Damon shrugged, "Sometimes Roosevelt makes no sense."

"Why did he keep Sam?" asked a dark-skinned stocky man.

"If I understand right, Roosevelt wanted him because is a seer. I believe he first tried to talk your friend into joining him. When that didn't work, he tried force and imprisonment."

The second guard came into the back, with bags of clothing. He passed them around until the prisoners each held their own.

"Where are our weapons?" asked the older woman, her steely gray eyes boring into him.

"Your weapons will be returned once we've reached your village," said Damon. "We'd like to get you home in one piece."

"How do we know this isn't a trick?" asked the older woman. "That you want us to take you to the village so you can wipe us all out?"

"Morrigu would never allow such a thing. Both she and Roosevelt have other fish to fry," said Damon.

"And she controls Roosevelt?" asked the older woman.

She was feisty.

"Not completely, but she has the ability to talk some sense into him," said Damon

He was done. Not going to discuss this any more. He gestured to the guards to herd them back into their cells to change.

"Bring them up when I call."

Damon took the elevator to the main floor and went

outside, the black van was already there. The driver, Eamon, Evangeline sitting in the seat opposite him, and the two guards seated in the back. Eamon opened the front, and only, door of the van. The black color of the van had turned yellow, covered with tree pollen. It coated everything this time of year.

Damon stood in the fresh morning air. He was tired. Wanted to sleep. Or at least, eat some breakfast. The wind blew past, promising more rain. He hoped the roads to the village were asphalt or concrete. He didn't want to be pushing the van out of a muddy rut.

The door opened behind him and one guard led the prisoners out, the other one followed. He carried five rifles, most with suppressors Damon noticed, and a bag of other weapons.

The old woman hopped on one leg, between the dark-skinned man and a blond woman, her arms over both their shoulders. Morrigu's doctor told Damon that he'd gotten a bullet out of the old woman's right thigh, It had been sewn up and bandaged. Luckily, nothing was broken and the arteries had been missed by the bullet. But that muscle would hurt for quite a while. The doctor had given her a pain killer, but that had probably worn off by now. Unfortunately, no one had been motivated to find her some crutches.

Two of the prisoners climbed into the black van and took seats. The other two who were helping the older woman, couldn't get her inside.

Damon said, "Allow me." He picked up the woman and carried her into the van and set her into a seat.

"Thank you," she said, looking flustered. He expected she wasn't used to being helped.

Damon dug into a pocket and took a pill out. He offered it to the woman.

"Now you're trying to poison me?" she asked.

"It's a painkiller. Won't knock you out or make you sleepy. These are what I use."

She glared at him, but took it anyway.

"For all I know, you're the one who shot me," she said, before swallowing the pill. "But thank you. Again."

"I wasn't part of that firefight. None of Morrigu's guards were. We weren't responsible for you getting shot." Then he straightened and said to everyone, "Now, can someone tell Eamon, our driver, where we're going?"

The tall Asian woman stood and walked up to the driver. They talked and she returned to her seat, moving with a grace he rarely saw in tall people. The guards had finished loading the villagers' weapons into the back, and closed the hatch.

Damon took a seat in the middle, across from the older woman. He buckled the seat belt. Many of the passengers weren't buckled in. Eamon turned on the engine and yelled, "Buckle up, everyone!"

Some did and the prisoners didn't.

Eamon stood and said, "This van doesn't move until everyone's buckled up." He waited until everyone was buckled up, then sat down and drove.

They went past the long row of warehouses, then cut right towards the front gate. Then right again, twice, driving north past the Zoo. A small plane landed on the runway. Another shipment, probably for Roosevelt. Morrigu didn't have anything scheduled today.

Eamon drove north for a mile or two, then turned off onto one of the small side roads. It was mostly asphalt. Where the road had buckled from the quake, someone had removed the broken asphalt and put gravel down. At least it wasn't completely muddy.

They drove past ruined, sagging houses. Tall trees and blackberry thickets filled what must have once been people's gardens. Nature reclaiming the land. Even the sidewalks had vanished beneath ivy. Damon had been told that the blackberries and ivy were imported from other countries. Out of their ecosystem, they had become invaders in their new home.

The van smelled stuffy, and full of unwashed bodies. Damon cracked a window, letting in the warm air of spring. The road was now completely gravel and just a bit wider than one lane. Damon didn't recognize anything.

How long had it been since he'd been outside the Zoo? He couldn't remember. Years? Decades? Probably the latter. Not since he was in his twenties. Before he'd sworn service to Morrigu.

Before then he'd drifted in and out of the Zoo. An orphan at 12, he'd been moved in with another family. They were deeply religious. He wasn't, and couldn't accept their deity being forced on him. So he'd run away to the Zoo. Joined a gang. Then switched to another gang. Ran with them for a while. Got sick of it all and left the Zoo. At twenty he'd tried to live in another village. To learn a trade. He wasn't any good at anything except fighting and he was still filled with so much anger. He went back to the Zoo, met Morrigu and his fate was sealed.

Even though he felt tired. He was getting too old to always be fighting. And Morrigu was headed for another war, perhaps two. At least she was avoiding one with the villagers.

The van passed through a hedge of blackberries and glossy-leaved bushes. There was only a foot on each side of the vehicle. It made Damon edgy. There was nowhere to turn around and run.

He glanced across the aisle. The woman was looking at him. He noticed she wore a large silver pendant in the form of a raven with Celtic knotwork. Something about it looked familiar.

"Do I know you?" he asked.

"I don't know. I know you."

"Where?"

"Back when you used to run with Scarecrow. I was with Blackjack. We used to fight a lot."

He looked at her more closely. Then he remembered. Her eyes and a knife flashing.

"You gave me this," he said, pulling up his sleeve to reveal a long ridged scar that ran the length of his forearm to his knuckles.

"I guess I did," she said.

"We've both changed a lot over the years."

"Yes."

"You got out of the Zoo."

"I was lucky. I didn't leave as smoke from ashes."

The Zoo had always burned their own and let the wind scatter the ashes where it would.

"Obviously, I'm still there," he said.

The van pulled up into a gravel turnaround overgrown with knee-high grasses and Eamon stopped the van, ready to exit the turn around. The road went no farther. Beyond large boulders, there was a footpath. A muddy footpath.

Eamon opened the door and said, "End of the line."

The four villagers got out and Damon carried the older woman out. He set her down and said, "Put your arm around my shoulder, I'll help you to your home."

"You've done enough," she said.

"I might as well. The other guards are coming to bring all your weapons. And some wine."

"You don't trust us?" She arched an eyebrow at him.

"Eamon doesn't trust anyone around his vehicles. Doesn't want anyone to shoot them up."

She laughed.

"What's your name," he asked.

"Cady."

"Cady. I don't remember ever hearing that name before, from when I was younger."

"I called myself Raven back then."

"Raven, I do remember hearing that. You were new to Blackjack's tribe. You were fierce."

"Still am," she glared at him. "I didn't stay with Blackjack long. After that I kept shifting to different gangs. Then fled altogether."

Three of the villagers were walking along the muddy path. Evangeline walked with them, talking to one of the men. She wore knee high black boots with no heels. The blond woman took Cady's other arm, putting it around her shoulder.

"I think I've got a pair of crutches that might fit you," the blond woman said. "We can stop by my place."

Between the two of them, they got her to the center of the village to be welcomed at the point of several guns.

The guards and Eamon came behind, with the weapons and a cart carrying the five cases of wine.

"It's okay," said the tall Asian woman.

"Who do these men belong to?" asked a tall man, holding a rifle.

"They work for Morrigu," she said. "She talked Roosevelt into releasing us."

"Is that who beat up Sam?" he asked.

Two of the other villagers were yelling, but Damon couldn't make out their words. He understood their intent though. They were angry.

This could go really wrong.

"Excuse me," he said. "We need to get Cady to her house. She's been seen to by a doctor, but she needs to lie down."

He nodded to Eamon, to continue the peacemaking.

Eamon was gifted at diplomacy.

"We come in peace, returning your people. Roosevelt has admitted he was in the wrong to take your people prisoner. That's a big step for him, I think. He had us bring five cases of his best wine as an apology."

"Why didn't he come himself," someone yelled.

"Because you'd shoot him," said Eamon.

"That we would," yelled someone else. The crowd laughed and weapons were lowered.

Damon took a deep breath.

Cady said, "My house is that way." She pointed towards the other side of the crowd.

"I think we should take you home, and then I'll go to my place and get the crutches," said the blond woman.

"Good idea," said Damon. "I think she needs to rest."

They moved through the crowd, who parted for them. Then past the center of the village, down a path. The village felt like none he'd been in before. It looked ramshackle, but he heard children laughing and singing. Adults laughed. There were animals everywhere. Chickens, cats, dogs. He heard goats, but didn't see them.

When he was a child, the village he'd lived in was joyless, gray and dismal. Everyone struggled. The other village he'd tried to fit into as a young man had been very rigid. He hadn't belonged in either one of those places.

In this village everyone looked well fed, healthy and fairly happy. Was it just the time difference, or was it just this place?

They walked past several houses and came to a small one. A huge black streak of cat shot into the house through a small door as they entered the clearing. Damon jumped in response.

Cady laughed. "Well, Monster's okay."

There were flowers everywhere here. Trees with pink blossoms and herbs growing in the ground. Damon had never seen any place like this. It looked like what paradise should look like.

The blond woman pulled the wooden door open with one hand and the three of them clumsily moved sideways through the door. The blond woman led them to the back of the small building, to a simple small bed with an iron frame.

How could anyone live in such a cramped space? Damon was used to living in Morrigu's warehouse, in a spacious room. Sparsely decorated with his narrow bed, a rack to hang clothes on and a small wooden table and wood chair. He didn't spend much time there. Morrigu kept him too busy.

How different Cady's life must be. A tiny house, a cat and a garden. How did she make her living? In the villages he was familiar with, people bartered to stay alive, or depended on their families. He didn't see much around here to barter with. The whole village looked to be full of gardens. Cady hadn't mentioned a family, but she'd left the Zoo long enough ago. She might have a family.

The blond woman helped Cady on to the bed and asked, "Can I get you some food? A cup of tea?

"Some tea would be good," said Cady.

The blond woman moved past him and went into the kitchen area.

"Are you going to be all right here?" asked Damon. "On your own?"

"Once Sharine brings me some crutches, I will."

Damon wanted to linger. He liked Cady. She was quick and smart. Strong and good company. When was the last time he'd simply sat and spoke with someone and enjoyed it? Well, no use going down that road. He'd chosen his path.

He should get back. Morrigu would need his help planning the trap for her competitors.

"I should go," said Damon. "Make sure the others aren't causing trouble."

"Thank you for bringing us home," said Cady.

The blond woman said nothing, her lips tight. As if to say that if Roosevelt hadn't taken their friend prisoner, it wouldn't have been necessary.

"It was the right thing to do," said Damon.

"Yes, but that rarely happens in the Zoo. In my experience."

"Things have changed a bit since your time there," said Damon.

"Not that much."

He nodded.

"If you ever want to leave," said Cady, "you know where we are."

He laughed.

"And how would I fit in here?" he asked, smiling.

"You must be able to do something useful," said Cady.

"I'd never be able to leave Morrigu," he said, sadly. "Not alive anyway."

He could smell mint, from the tea.

"If you believe you can't, then you can't," said Cady. "You're already defeated."

"True," he said. "I'll think about it."

He walked out the door and down the path to the main part of the village, feeling like he was closing a door. One he didn't want to close.

Focus.

Eamon and the others were clustered together, talking to two of the villagers. Their voices were calm, but Damon sensed Eamon's tension. Could read it in the way the man stood, ready to fight if need be. The other guards didn't look any more calm. Evangeline stood next to Eamon, watching and listening. Alert and ready for anything. Just like she always seemed to be.

He walked up to the group and said, "I'm ready to go."

Eamon nodded and said, "Nice talking to you folks. We'll take into advisement your warning."

"Do that," said the biggest guy with red hair and beard.

Damon looked at Eamon, who nodded and began to walk quickly back to the van. The crowd of villagers seemed to have dispersed, but he saw light glinting off a gun barrel behind a large tree. And another from around the side of a building.

They kept rapidly walking, Damon breathing deeply, trying to relax and stay as alert as possible. Ready to run.

Eamon hopped in the van and got it running. Everyone else hurried on board and took a seat. Eamon sped off down the gravel road. Damon heaved a deep sigh.

"What was the warning" asked Damon.

"Don't come back," said Eamon.

"Not likely," Damon said.

"I didn't think so, either."

Damon sat back in his seat and began mulling over possible traps for the Picasso thieves.

6

EVANGELINE

EVANGELINE STOOD OFF TO THE SIDE OF ROOSEVELT IN THE conference room. She wore stretchy tight black pants with a loose green shirt over a tank top and her holster. Around her thigh, was a sheathed knife. And her black boots. Her hair braided, as usual. She'd been considering shaving it all off. That was before she'd moved up here where it was cold all the time. She hadn't been warm since leaving Texas. She barely remembered Florida, but longed for the glorious heat and ease of her childhood.

The conference room was just a plain room in the top of the wine warehouse. Painted a drab gray color. Just like the skies here in this part of the world. She missed the sun. The room was furnished with a functional metal table and four metal folding chairs. Two of which barely held the bulk of Roosevelt and Young Roosevelt, who was old enough to be her grandfather.

The man was short, where his father was tall. Round and flabby, where his father was thick and muscular. But Young Roosevelt was quick-witted and sharp, on the surface. His father hid those skills beneath a layer of good-natured relaxation and joviality. Young Roosevelt was lighter skinned, much lighter. Leading Evangeline to think his mother might have been much, much lighter. She had never been mentioned by Roosevelt. Not once.

Roosevelt wore loose black pants and a deep purple shirt. Over those, he had on a black kaftan with red and gold braid at the cuffs and edges. He looked royal. Young Roosevelt wore a tailored black suit with tiny white stripes. What did they call that? He wore a black t-shirt beneath it and white shoes which stood out and looked rather silly.

She shifted her weight around a bit. She could see through an open window to down on the warehouse floor. Men were moving cases of wine, loading them onto a dolly to ready for shipping. She could hear the bottles clacking together within their boxes as each case was moved.

"Do you really need a bodyguard with me?" asked Young Roosevelt.

"She follows me everywhere, it's her job," said Roosevelt, as if just now noticing her.

"Get her a chair then," said the younger.

Roosevelt said to Evangeline, "Pull up a chair." He gestured to an empty chair at the table.

She quietly sat down in the hard, cold chair, feeling self-conscious. She didn't pull her chair up to the table. Sitting now, she could feel how much the bottoms of her feet hurt.

Her feet were swollen inside the tall black boots. The food she ate here was not agreeing with her. She should speak to the cook. Ask if she could get things her body liked. Less carbs, more protein and vegetables. There was hardly a vegetable on Roosevelt's tables.

"Relax," said Roosevelt, to her. "Rest. You'll need to be at your peak this afternoon. We're meeting with Morrigu again."

Evangeline took a deep breath and tried to slump in the chair. Her body didn't do relax. Not well, anyway. Sometimes, she wished it would. Then again, an easier life wouldn't fit her.

Young Roosevelt asked, "Why did you involve Morrigu in this, if you don't trust her?"

"Money. I don't have enough to take on the Eastside by myself. Art and jewelry are much more profitable than drugs and alcohol."

"So why didn't you take those, let her have the drugs and alcohol, way back when you split things up?" asked Young Roosevelt.

"She has the knowledge to deal with art and jewelry. I don't."

Young Roosevelt shrugged, sighed and said, "Okay, so we hit Morietti first. Why?"

"His territory is on the north edge of the Eastside. If we hit the strongest one, Collins, then we'd be boxed in on three sides by our enemies." Roosevelt pointed to a map that lay on the table in front of them. Each territory was outlined by a red pen and labeled with the name of who controlled it.

"What if the others band together though? They'd be stronger than just Collins. If we come in here, we drive a wedge through them. And take out the strongest of them. That might lead some of the others to cave, just out of fear. Offer them a decent deal, rather than have them fight you."

"But I can't ever trust them," said Roosevelt, taking a long draw on the beer that sat in front of him.

Evangeline could smell the bitter alcohol from where she sat.

"You don't have to trust them," said Young Roosevelt. "You need to get power over them and keep it that way."

"Ah, my son. Those are the old ways, I'm not sure they work anymore."

"Well, you do it by gaining their trust and making them love you. Make them want to serve you and reward them well for their trust."

"That's not how I work," said Roosevelt.

"You do that with your people," said Young Roosevelt.

"These are not my people."

"Once you conquer them, they're yours," said the younger, shrugging his shoulders.

Evangeline doubted that. It took more than conquering someone to gain their unwavering devotion. Still, Roosevelt did have a kind of charisma. He might be able to turn it to gaining people's trust. He'd gained her trust, despite Evangeline's oath to work only for women. She didn't trust many men. Didn't fully trust Roosevelt either, although she felt a loyalty to him. He'd been honest with her in a way most employers weren't. At least if he'd been lying, she hadn't yet discovered it.

"I'll think about this," said Roosevelt. "Take it to Morrigu this afternoon and get her opinion."

"Why?" asked Young Roosevelt.

"We need to tie her to this war. The more she's invested in it, the easier it will be to get the money, and her army."

"She won't want to take over? War Goddess and all."

"Not with pre-planning. Her wars were always more wild, free for all, kind of wars."

"I still don't think you should trust her. Getting her more involved will mean less control for you."

Evangeline watched Young Roosevelt. He was the heir of his father's empire, but appeared to be in no hurry to take over.

Was that a ruse or was it really who he was? Roosevelt hadn't mentioned that she needed to be on guard against him. Still, men had killed their fathers for much less than the power and wealth elder Roosevelt had.

Evangeline followed Roosevelt around the rest of the morning. She ate a rollup with chicken and greens in the empty hallway outside his room, while waiting for him to dress. Then she rode with him in the electric car to Morrigu's "palace."

The little black car drove itself between the two warehouses. There was only the one row of leather covered seats, to fit the two of them. They were wide and spacious, for a small car. Riding between the warehouse seemed silly on one hand. On the other, it meant Roosevelt could move quickly if there was trouble. Not many people knew the car could also fly short distances. The car looked cute and harmless. Not one that someone like him would usually use, thus it was useful camouflage. For public appearances, he used the sedan, which was bulletproof.

This time, Roosevelt and Morrigu met in a small room inside her warehouse, instead of the grand entry hall like before. The walls were realistic murals, painted like the trunks of trees, complete with bushes, birds and animal's eyes. The ceiling was a blue sky with a few clouds. The floor was painted brown with a stone path that led to the seating area of four chairs and a low table overflowing with pastries and fruit. Fancy teacups with saucers and a teapot sat on one end of the table.

There would be no space for Roosevelt's map. Wasn't this a working meeting? He'd certainly assumed it was.

Morrigu sat in an overstuffed chair, one leg draped over the arm of the chair and eating a bunch of grapes. She looked very relaxed.

Damon sat in a nearby chair. He looked anything but relaxed. Where was Santoni? Had the sorcerer been fired? No. Morrigu didn't fire people, Roosevelt had said. Had he been dispatched? He was a pathetic excuse for a sorcerer. But Damon had no magic she could sense.

Or did he have magic and was simply very good at hiding it? If so, why had Morrigu had Santoni there last time? Decoy? This was the part of her work she disliked the most. Trying to get a grounding in a client's normal life. And it appeared meetings with Morrigu were normal for Roosevelt.

Evangeline had only been with Roosevelt for two weeks. Barely gotten an understanding of who his own people were. Now, there were all of Morrigu's people to figure out. Evangeline felt completely out of her element here. She understood the environment in Florida where she'd grown up and Texas where she'd moved to, with her first boss, Mavis. Who died last month, of old age.

Roosevelt had caught Evangeline, unemployed and at loose ends, when he came to Mavis' funeral. So Evangeline had agreed to work for him. But this part of the world was unlike any place she'd ever been. The people so strange. She was used to the racial tensions of her previous posts. This felt like a military camp, but as far as she could see, the racial tensions were nonexistent. Either that or they were so far underground, Evangeline couldn't see them.

The mix here was mostly White, Hispanic, Black and Indian. With a few Asians: Chinese, Japanese, Vietnamese, and others she couldn't identify just by their names or their features. Possibly a mixture. There was very little pure blood of any racial strain these days. But she found it difficult to believe that race was unimportant here. Perhaps Roosevelt had screened people for bigotry. She'd have to ask him.

Morrigu called for another table for Roosevelt's map, which was brought in by a tall, muscular woman, who then left. So, it was going to be just the four of them.

"Sit down, please," said Roosevelt to her.

Evangeline opened her mouth to protest, then shut it again. He wouldn't have asked her to sit, unless it was important.

"I want you to see this map. To understand what we're up against," said Roosevelt. "It will be important in the future."

Evangeline sat in the chair next to him.

Morrigu said, "I think this is how we should proceed. I've sent Jeffries to find a job with Taylor's. He'll gather information and send it back to me. Then we'll decide how best to lure my enemies in and trap them. That's where I'll need your help. While Jeffries is gathering information, we should work on the problem with your competition. You have a map, that suggests a plan."

"I do," said Roosevelt. "I've talked with Young Roosevelt. We decided the wisest path is to attack my strongest competitor first. Rather than pick off the weaker ones first, giving the stronger one time to prepare for war."

"I agree," said Morrigu. "What do you need from me?"

"Collins' operation is bounded on three sides by my other rivals. To approach from those sides, we'd have to knock one of those out first. So our choices are to attack from the water, which is the fourth side, or from the air. The water side is probably heavily armed. I think we need an air attack. That will also let us remain invisible until we choose to reveal ourselves."

"Oh, I like that," said Morrigu, shifting in her chair, putting both feet on the ground.

Evangeline looked at Damon. His expression was unreadable. The man really bothered her. Too inscrutable. She liked to understand the people in the room.

"What do you think?" Roosevelt asked Evangeline.

"I have no idea," she said. "Warfare isn't my strong point."

"Damon?" asked Roosevelt.

"Do you have planes? Our shipping planes aren't exactly made for carrying bombs. And they certainly aren't armed with any type of gun."

"No, we would have to retool them," said Roosevelt.

"And what about your need for men?" asked Morrigu.

"I will need more. To mop up on the ground and to rein in my three other rivals," said Roosevelt. "I just don't have enough of an army."

"We can help," said Morrigu.

"Thank you," said Roosevelt, looking down and quite humble.

Interesting. Why the humble act?

Evangeline straightened in her chair, loosening up her muscles. More from habit than a need to stay alert. She didn't expect trouble. Didn't sense it either.

"What role will Evangeline be playing in this?" asked Morrigu.

"I'm not sure," said Roosevelt. "What can you do?"

Evangeline was taken aback. She'd never been part of a war. Her specialty was social functions. She was just a bodyguard, not a warrior.

Then it occurred to her.

"I could disguise the aircraft. For a time. I'm assuming your enemy has guns that could shoot them down. I think I would have to be on board one of them. To get close enough."

"Excellent," said Roosevelt.

"Will you be bringing the army in by aircraft or boats?" asked Morrigu.

"We don't control enough boats. That would get really messy. But to bring them in by aircraft would mean we'd need to capture a landing strip. Collins has one. But that complicates things," said Roosevelt, frowning.

"I have a few boats," said Morrigu. "I don't use them too often."

"You could bring in men with both planes and boats," said Damon. "That would strengthen your attack. We'd need to shield the boats from view. That might be difficult. I'm assuming their harbor is heavily armed."

"I'll have one of my pilots do a flight tomorrow. Just to nail down what we're up against. To make sure nothing's changed since the last time we looked," said Roosevelt.

"How long before the planes can be retooled?" asked Morrigu. She poured some of the hot coffee for herself. Leaving the others to serve themselves. Evangeline could smell the coffee and longed for some. But that would be too much. Sitting was distraction enough. She'd have coffee later. When she was alone.

"It will take two weeks to get everything in place. I need more weapons," said Roosevelt. "Will you be replacing your sorcerer?"

Morrigu frowned and said, "Good sorcerers are so hard to come by. I am searching. I can shield the boats from view."

Damon looked horrified.

"Don't say it," said Morrigu to Damon. "I'm perfectly

capable and I'll stay far offshore in a small, fast boat. Where no one can reach me."

Damon's face didn't change much, but Evangeline could tell he wasn't going to push it. Smart man. He knew when to be quiet. Still, if she'd been in his place, Evangeline would have been having kittens. Being a bodyguard was sometimes so frustrating when your employer persisted in putting themselves in danger.

Then again, Morrigu was a goddess. Could she even be killed? Evangeline didn't have any experience with trying to kill a goddess, and they all seemed to be so different concerning their strengths and powers.

Roosevelt poured himself a cup of coffee and took one of the scones. Damon did nothing. Just sat there. Alert for danger. Just like her. It was nice to know your competitor was a professional. If she ever had to fight him, it would be a real contest. Despite his age. Evangeline hoped it would never come to that.

"So, we're good to go in two weeks then," said Morrigu. "I'll send my Captain over to talk with yours. So the armies can train together."

"Good," said Roosevelt. "This is going to be fun." He licked his fingers from the pastry and rubbed his hands together like a little kid.

Evangeline swallowed. Her mouth felt dry, she was thirsty.

This was not going to be fun.

7

CADY

Cady sat outside in the spring sun. It wasn't completely warm, but she was working hard and only wore a long sleeved t-shirt, pants and her boots.

Someone had found a sturdy little metal wagon, made for a child. They'd fixed the rusted-out wheels, replaced them with new ones. She could sit on the wagon; her injured leg straight and resting, the other leg bent to wheel herself around the garden. Pulling weeds. She stretched down and pulled out a dandelion by the roots. She saved the dandelion roots for Sharine, who made medicine out of them. The greens Cady would use in a salad.

Her second crop of salad greens was coming up and being attacked by slugs. She needed to refill the beer traps, which were full of dead slugs and snails. Half a mind told her to borrow some of Joe's chickens. But they'd just tear up her greens with all their scratching. Or eat them.

It had been a week since she'd been shot. Her thigh still hurt far too much. At least it wasn't infected. She tried to rest her injury, but it was so hard to sit still when there was so much work to be done.

Gia came by every day, in her capacity as librarian. Bringing more books, trying to find one that would capture Cady enough she'd be content to sit in bed and read. So far it wasn't working.

Cady tried to push the wagon forward with her good leg. The wheels were stuck in a rut. Her blue shirt stuck to her skin, wet with sweat. On the third try, she got the wheels free and the wagon moved forward. Her muscles ached. She was getting old. And there was no safety net for her. Not without a family or friends. Why hadn't she thought to make friends? Now she could only hope for the kindness of people she barely knew.

Monster came out of the bushes and rubbed up against the bent leg. Her good leg. Then he leapt up onto her lap, purring madly.

"Why are you so affectionate all of a sudden? Worried I'm going to up and die on you? Silly cat."

Cady petted him and he lay down on her thighs. The big black cat had barely left her side since she'd returned. Maybe he was worried. Maybe it was because she was sitting or lying down most of the time. When she was up on the crutches he'd learned to stay away though. She was clumsy with them still. Hadn't realized how much upper body strength she'd lost over the years of soft living.

There was someone coming down the path. Limping.

As they came closer, Cady saw the bruised face and recognized Sam. So he was up and around. Good. Beth was due any second now. She'd need him to take care of the others.

"Cady?" he asked.

"Yes, hi Sam."

Monster looked at Sam, decided he wasn't a threat and closed his eyes, putting his head down and dozing, still on her lap.

"Aren't you supposed to be still in bed resting?" he asked.

"Probably, but I can't do that. It's driving me crazy."

He laughed, a surprisingly musical laugh. "Guess I can't either. I wanted to thank you for your part in comin' to get me."

"You're welcome. I'm glad to be able to do something to give back to the village."

"I can understand that. Sorry about your leg."

"It's not the worst that has ever happened to me," said Cady, laughing.

"If there's anything I can do to help. ..." he said.

"Looks like you're barely standing yourself. And you're going to have your hands full shortly, if they're not already."

"Oh, they are. Sarah's taken the little ones ever since I got back and Beth kicked me out of the house for the morning. Says she just needs to be alone. It's like this time she's even crazier than the last three." He grinned.

"Raging hormones, I expect. Which means she'll need you more than ever," said Cady.

"I know. But you clearly need some help. I wouldn't want you to lose your crops."

"So far, I'm doing okay. And the leg's healing. It's just a lot slower when you're old."

"How old are you?" he asked, grinning.

"Fifty, I think."

"Fifty. That's not old. Joe's sixty-five. Now that's old."

She laughed.

"Today, I feel eighty," she said.

"I hear you. But you're not to worry. I'll see to it that you're taken care of. I know you don't want to owe anybody anything. I'm guessing that's part of why you keep to yourself. And I don't know what your life was like in the Zoo, before you came here. You're one of us now. We'll do whatever we can to help you stay safe."

Cady felt her face flush with heat. No one had been this kind to her, not since she left the Zoo and her chosen family there.

"Thank you Sam. That means a lot to me."

"I guess we both had secrets to hide."

"Yeah. How are you going to deal with everyone knowing you can see possible futures?"

"I don't know. I'm still injured, so folks haven't been asking for help. I can't see into next week or two. My visions are farther out. But they're all telling me that there's going to be big shake-ups."

"Earthquake shake ups?" asked Cady.

"No power shake ups. War. At the Zoo. Surrounding areas, like here, are going to catch some of the fallout. I'm trying to think of how to keep us all safe. The visions aren't clear beyond the boundaries of the Zoo."

"Do the visions tell you when?"

"Well, Maddy looked older. Her face was thinner, maybe she's seven in the visions. So, maybe a year from now. Maybe a lot less."

"So, we've got a little bit of time. You should call a Council Meeting. More heads thinking about this will help."

"I plan on doing that. As soon as Sarah gives birth. I can't think about much else, till then."

"Understandable. But afterwards you'll be sleep-deprived. Your head won't be clear then, either."

"It's not clear now. The beating I took, it's made the visions more intense. I do know that you need to be at that meeting."

"Me? Why?"

"No one knows the Zoo better than you."

"I left the Zoo over twenty years ago. Everything's changed there. I'm of no use to you."

"You're one of the few people who understand how powerful Roosevelt and Morrigu are. And you know how to fight. You need to be there and talk to people. Some of them will want to rush in and fight. You know that. We can't win against the Zoo. We'll need your help. You are at the center of our survival. I have seen this. In every single vision. Not just one."

Cady didn't say anything. She closed her eyes and took a deep breath. Felt her energy ground itself, and looked deep within. *Do I get involved with this?*

You already are, came back the answer.

"I'll be at the meeting," she said.

8

DAMON

DAMON STOOD IN THE EMPTY GRAVEL PARKING LOT watching Roosevelt's new people spar with Morrigu's army. None of them had weapons. Some of Roosevelt's new people were experienced, most were not. It was probably pie in the sky thinking to hope they'd be fast learners.

Rain drizzled down his face. He shivered in the cold and acknowledged the ache in his left knee. The one that had been dislocated years ago. He slowly rolled his ankle in small circles. Moving the muscles. Warming them up without drawing attention to himself. He never counted on the advantage of people he worked with not coming back at him later as an enemy. No need to give away any of his weaknesses.

There. That one. The stocky guy with the pony tail. Using a martial move Damon had never seen before. The man took down an agile, muscular man larger than him. The fallen guy got up and went right back to it. They were fairly evenly matched on the surface of things. Except that the agile guy was breathing heavily and the stocky one wasn't winded at all. He was basically playing with the other man. The stocky one might be useful to put in a position of power. Maybe.

Damon paced up and down the line, watching Gregor, Morrigu's fight trainer, weave in and out through the sparring. The big man was keeping people in line. A couple of the new people, one man and one woman were clearly out to prove themselves. Out for blood. Neither had much control. Just rage. Although they did have some skill. If they could get their emotions under control, they might be good.

Then again, how many of them would be cannon fodder in a week?

He stopped pacing and glanced at the people fighting. This whole thing was a mess. No one, except maybe Morrigu had ever been in a large-scale war. None of them had been in an air fight. Or a battle on the water. There was no general, except Morrigu, who liked to wing it.

That made him very nervous. He needed to plan. It was his job to keep her safe, he couldn't do it with all this going on. He had never flown in a plane and didn't want to. Being out on the water scared him. The Salish Sound was too cold. Even if he could swim, hypothermia would kill him before he could get to shore. And who knew what was lurking beneath those waves. There were rumors of white sharks. Big ones. He shivered.

Morrigu had no general. She'd never needed one. She'd often led the skirmishes in the past, back when she and Roosevelt had been at war.

That was completely different. Both of them fighting over a small patch of land, that they knew intimately. It was close fighting. Knives and handguns, maybe a semi-automatic. Lots of ambushes and hand grenades.

Not the same as attacking an unknown enemy, who might

be armed better than you were since you just grabbed any weapon you could get your hands on. In a place where you didn't know the terrain, the buildings, nothing. Using planes and boats you weren't trained to use. Weapons you weren't familiar with. With no real battle plan.

It wouldn't work.

They needed a plan and it looked like no one was going to come up with one, except him. And there was also no sorcerer, other than Roosevelt's. Morrigu hadn't replaced Santoni and didn't seem to even be thinking about it. He needed to remind her to do that. Because Damon was sure that Collins had a sorcerer. Maybe more than one. He needed to find out more about Collins and get a feel for what they were up against. He might have to go on a flyover.

His wristband pinged.

Morrigu.

Damon sighed and left the training session, walking quickly past two of Morrigu's storage warehouses. He should call Gregor and put together a battle plan. The man was forever searching out and reading books about the old wars. Maybe he could help. Maybe he could do the flyover and see what Collin's weapons and security looked like.

He passed a guard, nodded at the woman, then pulled open the back door of Morrigu's Castle. From the sky above a roaring sound came. He couldn't place what it was. It didn't sound like the Zoo's cargo planes.

Then Damon saw sleek planes diving above Roosevelt's warehouses. Three of them. Dropping bombs and shooting big guns.

Within seconds Roosevelt's warehouses exploded, and went up in flames. The planes rose and leveled off, circling. Hopefully, just to see what damage had been done.

Damon was on his wristband.

"Everybody to the basement of the closest warehouse you can find. We're being bombed. Roosevelt's up in flames. Emergency communication only. Get inside and down."

He motioned to the guard to get inside.

His wristband was silent. As it should be.

One of the planes came back for another round, taking out the airfield. All of Roosevelt's modified for war cargo planes went up in fire and smoke. He could hear the explosions of the fuel tanks.

Damon coughed as the wind changed, bringing smoke his direction. He closed the door, but stayed outside. The breeze switched again and the air became more breathable.

The planes circled above.

He hoped the people sparring had gotten under cover in time. He couldn't see, there was too much smoke down here. All those warehouses of alcohol, and the weapons Roosevelt had been collecting, still exploding.

The planes must have been satisfied with the damage, they flew off. Towards the Eastside.

It must have been Collins. He was the only one over there with planes, their first reconnaissance flight had said. They must have been spotted. This was a warning.

If they'd been serious, every single warehouse in the Zoo would be gone. They'd known which ones were Roosevelt's and targeted those. They had someone inside.

Damon called Little Roosevelt on his wristband. There was no answer. He tried Roosevelt. No answer there either. Maybe their system had gone down with the bombing. He tried Evangeline.

"Here," she said, out of breath.

"What's your damage?" he asked.

"I don't know. I'm still off in the woods, outside the fence, gathering herbs. On my way back."

"Roosevelt's warehouses were bombed. Collins, I'm guessing. I can't reach Roosevelt or Little Roosevelt."

"Neither can I," she said. "Listen, I can talk to you or run fast. Not both."

"Okay. I'm going over there. Meet you there."

"Three minutes," she said.

Damon spoke to Morrigu's people with his wristband as he walked.

"Two of Roosevelt's warehouses have been bombed and shot up. And the airfield. I'm going over to see what's going on. I need about thirty strong backs right now. With stretchers. Get the medical center staffed up and running at full speed. We'll have casualties."

He felt rather than heard Morrigu's wave of rage. Damn, he'd forgotten about her. How could he have forgotten?

"We need to take care of our own first. Then decide how to respond," he sent to her alone.

Morrigu's voice was deep and controlled. "They will pay. Just not yet." He could sense the danger there. Relieved it wasn't aimed at him.

Damon ripped off part of his shirt and tied it over his nose and mouth.

The closer he got, the thicker the horrible, toxic smoke swirled through the air. He found people who'd staggered out of the nearby warehouses. The ones who hadn't gotten bombed. Air masks would help. Morrigu had none, at least not easily at hand. They hadn't been needed since the old days when she and Roosevelt were at war. Who knew what was in that smoke, could be poisonous gases.

He gathered together those still standing and able.

"You ten, get anyone alive to Morrigu's Blue Warehouse. Carry them if you have to. I've got people coming to help. The rest of you mask up however you can. We're going to the airfield to search for survivors. The warehouses are too hot. We'll have to wait till they burn themselves out."

They ran to the airfield. They found only four survivors. Two in the tower who'd been pierced by shattering glass and were bleeding badly. Two men who'd been unloading a jewelry shipment. Overcome by smoke and unable to hear from the explosions.

Some of the others carried the four wounded to the Blue Warehouse.

Damon looked around. All the planes on the ground were gone. Still burning, twisted piles of metal. The runway might be usable if it was cleared of rubble.

He'd have to get someone on that soon. At least two planes were scheduled to land this afternoon. If Collins didn't come back, they'd have at least two planes. Better tow them into a warehouse and hide them.

The large fuel tank was still burning, a column of black smoke spiraling into the sky. But the smaller one on the other side of the field looked untouched. It was underground and hopefully full.

Damon and the remaining people headed over to the Blue Warehouse. It was filled with people lying on empty pallets. Morrigu's medical staff, rushed around in their white coats. Doing triage. Morrigu walked between the pallets, stopping here or there.

He could feel her magic thick in the air, like tingling on the hairs on his arms and the back of his neck. She was either helping the healers or putting dying people out of their misery. He didn't have time to see which.

Damon pulled the cloth down off his face and gulped down the clean air. The ventilation system was running at full tilt. This had once been an art warehouse and air quality and temperature were important.

Damon motioned to anyone standing around.

"Back to Roosevelt's warehouses. Let's see if we can get in. Has anyone seen Roosevelt or Little Roosevelt?"

Everyone shook their heads no.

One of Roosevelt's men said, "They were both meeting in the munitions warehouse this morning. Taking stock of what we still needed."

That wasn't good.

The warehouses were still on fire. One of them, had partially collapsed. The other one looked dodgy, as if it could go down at any time.

Roosevelt's man pointed to the partially collapsed one and said, "That one's munitions. The one still standing held alcohol. Mostly wine."

Damon pulled thick leather gloves out of his pocket and tried the smaller door of the munitions warehouse. It creaked open. Heat and flames blew out through the open door. Damon leapt back.

Around the corner of the warehouse ran Evangeline.

"I can't get in from the other side," she said, winded. "Can't get the door open."

"Is anyone still alive in there?" asked Damon. "Can you tell?"

She stood and closed her eyes, gasping for breath. Searching. He could feel the magic roll off of her, like the sweat that trickled down her arms. She wore tight pants, boots and a t-shirt. A scarf around her nose and mouth. Her long braids tied back tight to her head.

She opened her eyes and said, "There might be one person alive in there. In the far back. But they're weak. I can't tell who it is."

"How about the other warehouse?" he said, nodding to the alcohol one.

She searched there and shook her head.

"No one."

Damon turned to the ten men behind him.

"Can we get those big doors open?" he asked.

"That would only fan the flames. We need to get the fire out," said one.

"Does Roosevelt have any fire fighting equipment?"

"We can link some hoses together. From water in the other alcohol warehouse. Might help a little," said another man, pointing to a warehouse next to the collapsing one.

"We should go in the front if we can," said Evangeline. "It's closer to the person who's alive. I think it's Roosevelt."

The man nodded, motioning to four others to follow him. They ran.

"Meet us in front! And someone find a sledgehammer fast!" yelled Damon.

One man ran off and Damon and Evangeline ran around the side of the burning warehouse. The heat was horrible. Damon hadn't thought he could run that fast anymore.

The two biggest guys took the door at the same time, but the lock held. Damn, steel door.

Evangeline tried to work on it with her magic, but it didn't budge.

"I can't do machines or mechanisms," she said, looking around wildly. "We don't have much time."

The man came back with a sledgehammer, breathing heavily. One of the big guys took it and pounded on the deadbolt with it. Finally, the lock gave and the door swung open. Smoke poured out. But there wasn't a fire in this end. It looked all metal and concrete. Not much to burn. There was nothing stored in this end of the warehouse.

"I'm going in," said Evangeline. "I can find him, but I won't be able to carry him by myself."

The two big guys said, "We'll follow."

She stepped inside the door, followed by them.

Damon told one of the others, "Go get a stretcher and strong backs to carry it."

If Roosevelt was alive, he'd need a stretcher. The man ran off towards the Blue Warehouse.

Then the other five men came back with the hoses and running water. They went inside and took turns shooting it towards the closest flames, trying to keep a safe path for the rescuers.

"C'mon, c'mon," said Damon to himself. This heap was going to collapse any moment.

9

EVANGELINE

Evangeline wove through the toxic smoke, the scarf still covering her mouth and nose. It wasn't helping much. Her eyes burned, and tears caused by the smoke ran down her cheeks, mingling with sweat.

She hurried, trying not to trip over all the debris on the floor. The smoke was so heavy that the fire wasn't lighting her way much. The skylights were useless. She trusted that the two men were able to see and follow her.

A faint pulse of life fluttered ahead, off to the left. The pillars of flames lit what was left of the warehouse. Periodic burst of gunfire sounded when a box of shells began to burn. Even more reason to hurry.

The ceiling creaked. It wouldn't last long.

Sweat ran into her eye and she wiped it away, surprised there was any liquid left in her body to sweat out. She'd run so fast from outside the fence. And then the unbearable heat from this fire.

There. Over by a still intact, pallet of guns. A dark shadow of a body lay crumpled. She ran to him. Roosevelt. The smoke was rising, down by the floor there was still clean air. But he was covered with blood.

The two men followed quickly and they straightened Roosevelt's body out. One of them quickly rolled on top of Roosevelt, grabbing one of Roosevelt's legs. The man pulled the leg up over his shoulder and continued rolling until he was on one foot and one knee. He balanced Roosevelt on top of his shoulders, then slowly stood. It was a move Evangeline had only witnessed once. Done smoothly and flawlessly.

The ceiling creaked again and the walls shuddered. Metal screeched.

The three of them ran for the exit. There was a path clear of flames where one of the men was using a hose. As Evangeline passed the man, she waved at him to leave, pointing to the ceiling.

They ran through the front door, the man carrying Roosevelt lagging behind. There was a stretcher there and two more men with it. They took Roosevelt from the big man's shoulders. The big man promptly collapsed. His buddy dragged him farther away from the building while the big man gasped for breath, recovering from the exertion, his shirt covered with Roosevelt's blood.

Evangeline ran a ways away from the building to where the others were. She ripped the cloth off her face and bent over double, breathing hard. Her lungs felt raw. Smoke was bad enough, but who knew what was in it. The bombs might have been filled with gas of some sort. Just the toxins from burning plastic were bad enough.

The men with the stretcher had put an oxygen mask on Roosevelt and were strapping him into the stretcher. It was one of those old ones, designed for rescuing people out in the woods. Made for carrying over rough terrain. They took off running before Evangeline could even get another look at Roosevelt to see how he was.

At that moment, the warehouse went down. The wave of heat and debris moved outwards like a cloud. They all ran farther away from the building. Even the big guy who'd been down.

Not long after, the alcohol warehouse came down.

Funeral pyres both of them. How many people had been killed? Little Roosevelt must be gone.

Damon said, "C'mon, let's go. Those of you who need to, go to Morrigu's Blue Warehouse. Let's get some water. Then we need to get the runway cleared. We've got two planes coming in today. They'll need a place to land."

He was right, but at that moment, she hated him.

Evangeline decided to go to the Blue Warehouse. Check on Roosevelt and get some oxygen. She was spent. Her muscles felt limp. After a rest, she would go help with the runway.

The others all went to find water and to help with the runway. She walked alone to the Blue Warehouse. The air was clearing a bit. The wind blowing the smoke off to the northeast. She just wanted to lie down and rest. Knew she needed to get her lungs cleared out.

The Blue Warehouse was organized. People all in white clothes, splattered with blood, moved between long tables stretching out across the floor. On top of those lay bodies. Live ones, she hoped. The place stank of fear and pain. Agony lay beneath those.

The large room was lit from overhead lights and big skylights. With the huge loading doors closed, Evangeline could smell the fresh air. They had a filter, which was clearing out any smoke that drifted in. Most everything looked clean.

One of Morrigu's people sat her down with an oxygen mask and water. The water was cold and tasted of minerals. She drank the entire large cup and asked for more, which was given. Her body was dehydrated. She could feel a headache coming on.

A woman in white quickly checked her. Then she rinsed her eyes with a saline solution which felt cool and healing.

"Sit here for a few minutes. Get your lungs cleared out. Rehydrate," was the woman's final decision.

She glanced over to the table where Roosevelt lay. Surrounded by medical people. Morrigu stood nearby, doing powerful magic.

There was nothing Evangeline could do to help. She didn't have much healing magic, even on a good day. This was no longer a good day.

So, she sat and breathed the clean oxygen into her raw lungs. Her throat hurt, too. She took the mask off and gulped down more water. Then put it back on and breathed deeply, appreciating the pure air.

Where did they get oxygen from? How did they extract everything else out of the air? Sometimes she marveled at the tech that still existed after all this time. Her world hadn't added much to the repository of information. Neither had the last few generations. They'd simply been trying to survive.

How many people had been lost in this raid? Would Roosevelt want revenge? Evangeline would if she were him. It was most likely that Young Roosevelt was dead. It would take a lot of effort to find his body, if it wasn't totally incinerated. What did these people do with their dead?

Evangeline became aware of a shadow hovering over her. She looked up to see Morrigu.

"How is he?" asked Evangeline.

"He will live, but it will be a very long time before he will be able to run his business again. If ever," said Morrigu, in a quiet, sad voice. Unlike one Evangeline had ever heard her use.

"How long?"

"I do not know. He is not awake. His heart stopped for a time, but it is beating again. The doctors may be able to tell you more when they are finished with him. He would be dead if he hadn't been brought here when he was."

"He was the only one still alive in that warehouse. Too many things exploding."

"Oh, so that's why his ears felt all puffy. They were damaged from the noise," said Morrigu, sitting down next to Evangeline.

"He was in the munitions warehouse when it was bombed. When we went in to get him, there were still cases of ammo catching fire and exploding. After we got him out, the roof caved in and the whole building went."

Morrigu shook her head. She put a hand on Evangeline's. Morrigu's hand felt hot, burning with energy.

"I will see that Collins pays for the deaths and damage he's created. I cannot say when. Damon is better at gauging that sort of thing. But Collins will pay. An attack on Roosevelt is an attack on me. And never has Morrigu not sought revenge. Collins will find that he's underestimated me. Will you join me?"

"I am under contract to Roosevelt."

"I do not think he will need you in the near future. Should he live, he will not be able to communicate with anyone for quite some time."

"I will need to think about it," said Evangeline. "I'll have questions. Right now my mind isn't clear enough."

"I understand. I'm ready to answer questions when you have them. For now, heal yourself. Get some rest."

Morrigu stood and walked away. Back to the people still laying on tables. Healing some, putting others out of their misery. Giving them quick, painless deaths.

Evangeline searched her feelings for a path to follow. Nothing was clear. Everything was a fog today. She didn't need to decide now.

The doctors still surrounded Roosevelt. There was nothing she could do here.

She finished her glass of water. Took one last deep breath of oxygen. Then unzipped the pockets in her leather boots and took out the thin leather gloves, zipping the pockets again. She put the gloves on and stood.

She'd go help with the runway and then return to the woods outside the fence. Pick up her bag of herbs she'd been collecting. Then get some food and call it a day.

Before she went out the door, Evangeline turned. Near Roosevelt's bed stood a tall black man in a red and black pin-striped suit. A red tie. His long shimmery braid reached mid-chest. His skin darker than Roosevelt's. The man had a cigar in his mouth, but no smoke came out. His eyes met hers and he held up a hand. In his fingers were green leaves. She couldn't tell what they were from this distance. The expression on the man's face was grim. Sad.

It took her a full minute to realize it was Kalfu. There were rumors that Roosevelt followed him. Making use of Kalfu's dark magic. Evangeline hadn't really believed it. But there he stood, no mistaking it. Kalfu and Morrigu. Dark aspects both.

When she looked back, Kalfu was gone. Evangeline shivered and went out the door into the blinding sunlight.

There were seven of Morrigu's men at the runway,

including Damon. Moving big chunks of asphalt by hand. The single tractor in sight was a mangled piece of metal.

Evangeline helped as best she could. She was strong at least. Although she was the first to flag. After they'd cleared a few meters, Damon handed her a metal rake.

"This needs to be raked fairly level."

She went to work. Smoothing the bare soil where the broken asphalt was removed. By the time they'd finished what Damon deemed a long enough strip, a plane was buzzing overhead.

Evangeline had a moment of panic at the thought of another attack. Then it passed. This plane was much clunkier looking than Collins' planes had been. It was a cargo plane.

"Outta the way everybody!" yelled Damon.

He waved his arms in a sweeping "here you are gesture" and backed away from the runway.

The plane landed, bumpily, and came to a stop at the very end of the area they'd cleared.

The pilot opened his door and asked, "What the hell happened here? There's no radio. No runway." He was a young, red-headed man. Pale and anxious.

"We got attacked. C'mon. We've got to get your plane off the runway. We still have another one coming in today."

The pilot went back inside the small plane and pulled out a metal tool. He hooked one end to the front wheels of the plane and took the handle. It had a battery pack and he turned it on, pushing the plane off the cleared runway towards the warehouses. About twelve meters. Giving another plane enough space to land.

Damon handed the rake to one of the men, who raked down the runway again. Flattening it where the plane had dug up some dirt.

The other men helped unload the plane. It wasn't carrying much. Just a couple of paintings.

"We've got to get that warehouse cleared," said Damon. "Everything moved out, so we can move the plane in there. If Collins does another flyover, let him think he destroyed all our planes."

The pilot nodded and said, "Helluva thing. Looks bad from the air."

"It is bad," said Damon.

The pilot went back and got his gear out of the plane, closing the doors and patting his plane, before heading off towards the warehouse.

"Are you done with me?" asked Evangeline.

"Yeah. I'll get some of the other workers to move the warehouse contents. You got things to do?"

"I need to go back outside the fence. Get the herbs I collected. I left them when all this blew up."

"Take someone with you," said Damon.

"What? Why? You think I can't defend myself?"

"No. We just need people to keep an eye on each other. There's less chance of anyone sneaking up on two people than one. I'm not sure Collins won't follow up with a ground attack. They could be out there in the woods waiting right now."

"Waiting for what? We just passed our weakest point. We've had time to get the injured to medical. The warehouses have collapsed. Now we're mopping up."

"We're distracted. Not expecting another attack. Take someone with you. Someone with a functioning wristband. And don't go out of range."

She saw his point, but didn't like his tone.

"All right. I'll go get one of Roosevelt's guards who's off duty. That okay?"

"Perfect."

"You know Morrigu asked me to work for her."

"Doesn't surprise me. She fired Santoni. He was worthless. She needs a sorcerer."

"If I decide to work for her, and that's a big if, I won't take orders from you. Not with that tone. I don't take shit from anyone." Not like she used to.

"I'm sorry. It's been a bad day. I'm not at my best," said Damon. "I should have foreseen this. We shouldn't have done two flyovers. One was risky enough."

"Roosevelt was the one who demanded two, wasn't he?" she asked.

"Yes. I should have said no."

"Not your call," said Evangeline. "Let it go. Nothing to do about it now."

"You're right," Damon said.

"I'm always right," she said.

Then walked towards Roosevelt's home warehouse. Hopefully, one of the guards would be there. Damon was right. The woods could be filled with Collins' people by now.

10

CADY

CADY STOOD IN HER DOORWAY, HER ARMS OVER THE crutches, looking at the sky. It was gray. Still filled with smoke and toxic chemicals from yesterday. She'd seen the planes flying away from the Zoo after the huge explosions.

Bombs, she guessed, although one had never gone off in her lifetime. Not big ones like that. There hadn't been a mushroom cloud, those were the really bad ones. Or so she'd been told.

Then Cady had seen the columns of black smoke coming from the direction of the Zoo. The explosions had rocked the village and her little house so hard, she'd almost taken it for a quake.

What had happened there? She and the other villagers were burning to know. None of them willing to go look, except a couple of young fools. They'd taken off on foot last night at sunset. They should be back by now, but Cady hadn't seen them yet. Her house was apart from the rest of the village. Surrounded by trees and huge bushes.

She shifted her weight. The leg was healing, but not fast

enough to suit her. She still couldn't walk without the crutches. It hurt too much. Sharine had told her to give it another week. Not to rush things.

The dry season was here. She couldn't water her garden without the help of her neighbors, who took turns coming to help her water. Which irked her. She'd never needed anyone's help before.

But it wasn't even that. It meant that someone was always coming around to check on her. To make sure she was all right. And the people always talked to her. They interrupted her solitude.

She missed being able to go days without seeing a single person. Of having the only voices she heard being those of the birds, frogs and the wind. Of being able to see deities traveling through the woods.

Now there was too much clutter in her mind. Other people's voices. Telling her about this one's troubles with their children, or another one's problems with a lover. Or those two's argument about the way to cook a piece of meat.

They meant well, the villagers' did, but they tired her. All of them chattering away so much. And she was so grateful for the help with her garden and the food they brought. But, since she'd left the Zoo and come here, solitude had allowed her to heal. To hear the small voice inside herself and follow its lead. Which had brought her to finding peace. She rather liked it.

Sharine walked into the clearing in front of Cady's house.

"You're up and about. Good. How's your leg doing?"

"About as well as can be expected. Healing. Slowly."

"Well, our bodies heal slower as we age."

"Frustrating."

"Yes. Mateo and Will are back. They're about ready to tell everyone what they found. I thought you might like to hear."

Damn. Cady *was* curious.

"All right, I'll come."

Cady left the doorway of her house, slowly going down the one concrete step to the ground. Didn't want to fall and have another injury. She hobbled along with Sharine back to the center of the village. Even though Sharine walked slowly, Cady was breathing hard when she got to the meeting place. Using crutches was hard work. At least they'd get her in better shape. Her arm muscles were gaining strength by the day.

Gia saw her coming and got up from a wooden chair someone had brought out and motioned for Cady to sit. She did, not feeling guilty at all.

Joe, Cady's closest neighbor came running up, out of breath.

"Sorry, one of the baby goats was tangled up in wire from the chicken pen and I had to get it loose."

Mateo walked to the center and began talking. "Okay. Everyone's here. So Will and I left late last night. Walked to the Zoo. Didn't run into any problems. The Zoo was mostly lit up. Huge overhead lights on large metal poles, like the ones you find in a lot of what used to be the city. Except the ones at the Zoo work. They give off a lot of light, almost as good as broad daylight with that full moon last night. There were a lot of guards out, so we never left the woods. Didn't want to get shot.'

"We could see that two huge warehouses had been bombed and collapsed. Smoke still coming from them, although people were trying to pull debris off the heap of wreckage. Off one of the buildings. The other they stayed away from. Every now and then we heard a lot of bullets exploding from that collapsed building. Anyone working close to it ran away. I'm guessing they had a lot of ammunition and weapons stored in that warehouse and some of it's still catching fire and going off."

"Wasn't anyone trying to put the fires out?" asked Mazzy.

"They had a couple of hoses running, trying to put them out. But they didn't seem to be making much progress," said Will. "The fire was too big."

Cady hoped that Damon hadn't been in one of those warehouses. She quite liked him. He was someone she could have been friends with. Not that she'd ever see him again. He'd never leave the Zoo, not alive at least.

Mateo said, "We could see clear across to the other side, where the airfield is. The tower was a heap of rubble. And at least eight, maybe more, planes were destroyed. There were piles of concrete over by the runway, like it had been bombed, too. No workable planes in sight."

There was mumbling between the villagers.

"What do you think happened?" asked Beth.

"They pissed somebody off," said Will.

"Are we in danger?" asked Beth.

Everyone looked at Cady, as if she had the answer.

Cady said, "If they were attacked, Morrigu will attack back. If their enemy isn't completely destroyed, there will be war. Morrigu is a war goddess. And Roosevelt follows Kalfu. They won't be content until they have revenge."

"So war might spill over into the surrounding areas," said Beth.

"Might," said Cady.

"Will," said Sam.

Everyone turned to look at him.

"I've seen war come here. Our houses here burning. In our lifetime."

"What can we do to prepare?" asked Mazzy.

Sam shrugged, his face looked haunted.

"Move," said Sam.

"No," said Joe. "We've got fresh, clean water here. Might not find that anywhere else."

"He's got a point," said Brady. "It's easier for those of you who don't work the land to move, than me. I've spent ten years creating deep, rich loam to grow food in. Food that feeds at least half this village."

"What are our alternatives?" asked Mazzy. "Build defenses?"

"Walls won't do much good if we're attacked from the air," said Will.

"Can we dig underground? Make some sort of shelter far below ground?" asked Mazzy.

"That's possible," said Will. "It probably wouldn't stand up to a quake, so we'd have to keep a close eye on it. But it might save our lives."

"I think we should do two things," said Mazzy. "Brady and Joaquin and anyone else interested should scout out a new home for us. One with plenty of fresh water and good soil. Will and Ryan, start exploring some high ground. A place where we might dig a shelter that won't flood. How does that sound to everyone? We think about this first before we act. For at least a week. Make a smart decision."

The entire village agreed. That didn't happen often.

For the next week the village was a noisy place. People came to visit her every day. Speculating on whether they'd move or dig in. Brady had been sent northeast with two other men and Joaquin had gone northwest with Sam and Gia, who both thought that was a more likely direction to find water and perhaps empty land.

Will and Ryan were searching for ground high enough to

dig down and build a shelter. The water level got pretty high in the village during the winter.

They couldn't move until Brady's crops came in, that was for sure. If Sam had said they should move, Cady was all for that. She'd be sad to leave her lovely home, but if he'd seen it in his visions, then he'd seen it.

People were already beginning to build carts for their chickens and necessary belongings. Moving an entire village miles away wouldn't be easy. Not without roads.

She looked at her books, patting each one. She might take one or two of the small ones. That would be it.

She couldn't decide about Monster. He'd become even more friendly now that she was sitting so much. He'd even jumped up and sat in her lap a few times. She should bring him along. Maybe she could get someone to build a cage for him. He'd hate her for that, though. Would it be better to just leave him to fend for himself?

She didn't have an answer.

Five days later, Will and Ryan gave up. They couldn't find high enough ground to build a shelter except for miles away. Too far away to make it usable.

Six days later, Brady and the other two men returned. They had found one small stream, but the plants all along it were withered and weak as if they were slowly being poisoned. The soil nearby was poor. It was covered mostly with asphalt and decaying or collapsed buildings. They met quite a few scattered groups of people, none of them friendly.

Things weren't looking good.

Joaquin, Sam and Gia returned after a week. They found two lakes. One was surrounded by a fairly large village. The village was prosperous and friendly, but there wasn't enough usable land to absorb another village. They'd fed

Joaquin, Sam and Gia and proudly showed off their own village. Then pointed them in the direction of another, nearby lake, which the three went off to investigate.

That lake was unoccupied by people. There would be a lot of work to do. All the houses built there were too far gone to use, but the water was clean, the soil good. There was a forest nearby with enough wood to build homes from. And the lake had fish.

There was no choice to be made, other than to stay or go.

The village voted to go, unanimously, although everyone had regrets.

Joaquin, Ryan, Tank, Bao, Will, Brady and Mateo left for the lake. Joaquin to guide them. Ryan, Tank, Will and Mateo to begin building houses. Brady and Bao to ready the soil and plant fall crops.

Everyone else began packing. They would begin to leave in two weeks, after harvesting. It would take at least a day, perhaps more to move. There were no usable roads and they had to detour around places where the people were unfriendly.

Cady found an old bike. Joe made boxes, out of wire, to put onto it that would hold her belongings. She couldn't ride it, not on the trail they'd use, but she could wheel it. She didn't know how to ride a bicycle anyway. Silly things. Joe added an extra wheel in the back for balance. The bike wouldn't fall over anymore.

Cady hoped she could walk by then. She didn't have much to bring. A few clothes. The blankets on her bed, one of them newly woven, a gift from Sarah for bringing Sam home. Her box of weapons, although she should put them in a bag. It would be lighter. Herbs she'd harvested from her garden and dried. Plus seeds from some plants and roots of others wrapped in wet cloth. Any food from her garden. That was about it. Very few belongings for fifty years or so. Then again, she'd never been one to collect much.

She needed to make a decision about Monster.

That night when he came inside and jumped up on her lap as she sat reading in bed, she petted him and said, "My friend, I'm moving. Going to a new home, along with the rest of the village. You have a choice. You can either come with us, riding in a cage, or stay here alone. You have to make the choice, I can't do it for you. Won't do it for you."

Monster purred and purred. Then curled up on the bed and stayed the whole night. And every night afterwards.

"So be it."

Cady mentioned it to Sharine when she came to collect the crutches.

"I've got just the thing for you to carry him in. It's made of hard plastic and metal. Made to carry pets in, I think. It's very old, but it still works. You can drape a cloth over it to give him some shade and make him feel safer. I've also got a harness and leash. You might be able to train him to wear that. Maybe. I've read of such things."

"I'll try both. See which works better."

Despite the sadness of leaving her perfect home, Cady was looking forward to the adventure of a new life. She had grown to quite like the people in her village.

Cady was bent over, tying a strip of cloth around the stem of an oregano plant to mark it. The scent of the pungent herb rose to her nose. She'd marked most of the plants she wanted to take chunks of. Wouldn't dig them till the very last minute. Fall was a good time to transplant, but she'd need to water things well in the new village until the rains came. Each year they seemed to come a little later.

She heard a loud rustling in the big leaf maple overhead. Dead branchlets fell to the ground. She looked up to see a dark shadow which startled her. A large, dark shadow.

"Now who are you?" she asked, not expecting a reply.

The shadow rustled again, as if trying to balance itself in a too small space. Then a long thin neck with a reptilian head moved outward and down, gazing at her.

"I am called Onyx, if you must know," it said, with a gravelly voice, as if it hadn't been spoken to for a very long time.

It was a dragon and looked like the same one she'd ridden on in her journey, searching for Sam. Did all dragons look alike? Except this was no journey. She was standing here, in her garden, completely present, in broad daylight. Monster sat at her feet, looking up. Warily, but not afraid.

"Are you real?"

"Am I real? Of course I'm real. What else would I be?" The dragon fluttered its wings.

"Why are you up in a tree?" she asked. Not willing to end the conversation. Unsure if the dragon was dangerous. It was huge.

"The view is very nice from up here. And there aren't many places to land near your house. Not without me crushing everything."

"Very thoughtful of you. You could land near my front porch. The hydrangeas will recover."

"Thank you," it said. "This tree isn't quite large enough for me."

The dragon flew off the branch and landed gracefully in the small space in front of her house. She hadn't done much to clear the woodland around it. Just carved out a small space to garden and a few paths.

"Why are you here?" she asked, walking a bit closer. Monster stayed behind her, a wary eye on the dragon. If Monster could see it, then it must be real.

"I came because you need me."

"Why?" What on earth did she need a dragon for?

"I don't really know. I thought you would know."

"I didn't even know dragons existed in our world."

The creature's body alone took up the entire empty space in front of her house. Over three meters long and its back just as high. The tail was wrapped neatly around its feet. The dragon had shiny scales that held a multitude of colors as they shimmered in the sunlight. Its neck looked to be as long as the tail, and on the end of it was a graceful head with fleshy protrusions that flared back along the neck, turning into a wavy ridge that continued on the back to the tip of the tail. The chin had similar protrusions, but smaller, to form a beard. Large silky-metallic wings were folded curved against its body. Its large eyes were the color of dark yellow marigolds.

"Deities didn't exist in this world until recently either, not really. Most people don't believe we dragons exist. They have no trouble meeting a unicorn or Krishna, but a dragon. Impossible!"

"Where are you from?"

"I was sleeping beneath a mountain. In a lava tube that was warm and cozy. I woke up because I felt needed. It took me a few weeks to get here. I hadn't eaten in centuries. We don't when we're sleeping. So, I had to gain some strength before I could come find you. And I had to find a secluded lake to bathe in."

"What do you eat?"

"Everything. Deer, goats, sheep, willows. Berry brambles, which are especially good this time of year around here, because they are filled with berries. I sometimes eat fish, but they're not my favorite."

"But not people."

"I have never tried eating people. The clothes would be too much work to get off. And I like it when people talk to me. Eating them or threatening to sort of ruins all that."

"I have no idea why you were called."

"There is danger, that's why."

"The whole village is in danger."

"Well, tell me about it," said Onyx, lying down and tucking its paws in. Just like a cat.

So, Cady filled Onyx in on the Zoo, the impending war and the village's plan to move.

Having no idea why a dragon might have been called. Maybe it hadn't been her who called. Or perhaps it had something to do with that journey to find Sam and the black dragon who came for that journey. The journey to the Zoo to see if Sam was still alive had been a vision, her soul leaving her body. Had that dragon been Onyx's soul? Did dragons have souls? Probably, she decided.

As she talked, Monster went up to the dragon and sniffed it. Then must have decided the dragon was safe. The cat climbed up onto its paws and curled up to sleep in the sun.

When Cady finished, Onyx looked thoughtful. At least that's what Cady decided it was doing.

"I think you must need me for your trip to your new home. And perhaps to keep the new village safe. I can do that. You'd better warn the other villagers about me though. Not all humans are accepting. Not all of them can travel other realms like you."

"I can only journey to find things, not any other time. I'm not like Sam who sees visions."

"Tish tosh. You build fences where there are none, but that is a matter for another time. We will talk of it on a deep winter's night in front of a warm fire. You should tell the gossip mill about me."

"Gossip mill?"

"The two or three people in the village who spread gossip around."

"I have no idea who that is."

"Well, then tell them all. Before anyone tries to attack me. I'll wait here, with your cuddly cat. I need a nap, too. I've had a long journey to get here."

With that, Onyx stretched out its neck and lay the graceful head down. All without Monster waking. Soon, the dragon began to snore.

Cady shook her head in wonder. She walked around the great beast, having to touch the smooth, shiny scales as she walked between it and her house to the path leading into the rest of the village. They would never believe her. Until they saw him. Maybe she should start with Joe, since he was her nearest neighbor.

Joe was nowhere to be found, so she continued on into the village, her injured leg now just a slight limp. She was getting better, slowly.

Several women sat in the center of the village, in the shade of the large oak tree. Spinning, or knitting, or doing other portable work. Children played in three different groups, divided mostly by age.

"Cady, how are you?" asked Mazzy.

"Confused."

"Why?" asked Sarah.

"I have something to announce. And you are all going to

think I'm crazy, but I'm not," she said, standing there, feeling like an awkward teenager.

"Okay," said Mazzy. "Announce away."

"I have a guest. A rather large guest, who plans on accompanying us on our journey to the new village. And possibly staying."

"That's not a problem," said Mazzy. "You know the village rules. Harm no one and be kind. If your guest can abide by those, they're welcome."

"I didn't bring that up to it yet. My guest is rather unusual. Its name is Onyx. It's a dragon."

"A what?" asked Sarah.

"I told you that you'd think I was crazy. It's a dragon."

"Dragons don't exist," said Sarah. "Only in stories."

"Neither does Morrigu, but Mazzy saw her when we went to the Zoo. Neither does Diana, but she walked through the middle of the village two days ago. What didn't exist is alive and well in our time."

"Okay," said Mazzy. "Does it mean us any harm?"

"No. Onyx wants to help. To protect us."

"From what?" asked Sarah.

"I don't know, neither does Onyx. Maybe from the Zoo, the war or maybe something we don't even know about," said Cady.

Mazzy took a deep breath and said, "I want to meet this dragon."

Cady could tell the woman was terrified.

Why hadn't she been terrified? She'd been startled to see his huge bulk in the trees above her. Then a bit alarmed when it was down on the ground in front of her house and she could see how large the dragon was. But somehow terrified hadn't entered the picture. She hadn't even looked around for a weapon.

She hadn't sensed danger from the dragon. Onyx had done everything possible to make itself look smaller and seem harmless.

"Well, let's go," said Cady.

She was followed by everyone gathered nearby, and a few others who came running when called.

11

DAMON

DAMON SAT AT A ROUND TABLE IN THE SMALL UPSTAIRS room of Morrigu's Art Warehouse 3. There were three of Roosevelt's advisors: Jack, Ethan and Avery, Gregor, Morrigu's Fight Trainer, Evangeline and Morrigu. Seven of them, all trying to decide the fate of the Zoo.

Roosevelt was conscious now, two days after the attack, but he still couldn't hear. Or speak. He was cut up and badly burned. They'd found a lot of bodies in the past couple of days, buried beneath the debris of the warehouses. Someone had identified Young Roosevelt by a ring he wore, which was found near something that could have been a body. There were bones there at least. Not much left resembling a human after all the bombs, explosives within the warehouse, and the fire.

The last two days had been hell. Damon hadn't slept for days and was running on coffee. And occasionally food when someone shoved a plate in front of him, demanding he eat.

They'd bury the bodies this afternoon. Over near the fence. In a mass grave with a tree planted on top. Normally, the Zoo burned their dead, but no one could face another fire.

Damon sipped coffee and listened to the bickering, his stomach roiling from too much coffee. It wasn't a question of whether to attack Collins or not. It was when. Now or wait.

He ran his hands through his hair. No one had even considered not attacking. Not retaliating.

He looked up to see Morrigu staring at him. She was annoyed. Probably because she wanted to attack tomorrow. Roosevelt's advisors knew there were no weapons to attack with. Nothing that would match Collins' arsenal anyway. They knew waiting was important.

"Damon, what are your thoughts?"

The room quieted.

Damon said, "I think we need to find Collins' spy first. Hopefully, he's not one of us in this room. It does us no good to make plans if Collins knows we're doing that. Personally, I don't want a war. I've been at war and I don't ever want to be there again. Not at this scale."

"So you won't fight in this war?" asked Morrigu, her voice cold.

"Of course I will. You asked my thoughts. I won't lie to you. I don't think we have the people or arms to match Collins. We're weak and he's strong. From what I understand, he's spent the last few decades fighting his neighbors. Building up an army and weapons. Roosevelt's spent the last month or two caching weapons, nearly all of which have been destroyed. We're down to two planes, which will barely keep your business alive and the money flowing in. We've lost at least thirty people in the attack. At least that many have now fled. They were people who aren't fighters, warehouse workers, cooks and cleaners, people who want no part in this war. We don't have enough warriors to fight. And those we do have aren't trained well enough." Damon looked at Gregor.

Gregor nodded. "It's true. Nearly all of them need more practice. And there aren't enough."

Damon said, "First we must find Collins' spy."

"How do we do that?" asked Avery, rubbing her short-cropped, black hair. "We didn't even know there was a spy. Until the attack."

"Anybody new show up in the last couple of months? Someone who seems eager to impress? A little too eager? Someone who wasn't around during the attack? Anyone disappear just before the attack and not return?" asked Damon.

Gregor said, "A lot of the people I've been training are new."

"Did any of them have access to the arms warehouse?"

"No," said Jack, his small frame with its compact muscles leaned forward over the table.

Damon had never seen the man not look tense.

Jack said, "They haven't been around that long. And the people who did have access to that warehouse know to be silent about it. It's a restricted area. We don't talk about what's in there or even which warehouse the weapons are in."

"So maybe it's not someone new," said Ethan, pushing his bulk away from the table. He was a large, heavily muscled man.

"Maybe not," said Avery. "We still don't have a complete list of bodies yet. We're still trying to ID them all."

"Not an easy thing," said Damon. "I still don't think we can make any move at all until we know who this person is. And make sure they're the only plant Collins put in our organization."

"I think you're right," said Jack.

"We've got to keep training," said Gregor. "And increasing

our army and our weapons. Slowly. And without drawing attention to those looking. We don't have enough people to fight a war, or get revenge."

"It only takes one person to get revenge," said Morrigu.

Damon stared at her. What did she have in mind?

"Can you elaborate on that?" he asked.

Morrigu shrugged, "It's simple. We don't have to fight a war. We just have to kill Collins.That only takes one person. A person with skill, who can get close to him and kill him."

Damon said, "He may have his empire set up in such a way that there's a successor. Who might be worse than him. And who would go all out after us."

"Well then, you'd better figure out a solution. Because revenge is going to be mine. Somehow, someway. I'm willing to wait, for months perhaps. First we find any spies and you can give them to me. I'll make an example out of them that no one will forget. And we'll make sure Collins knows about it. But then, I will take from him all those he loves."

With that, Morrigu stood and swept out of the room.

Damon was shaking inside, but refused to let it show. Morrigu meant what she said. He almost felt sorry for Collins.

Damon sighed and asked, "Anything else, anyone?"

Everyone shook their heads.

"Good. We'll meet here tomorrow morning. I want a report of who's missing and when they left, as well as who's dead. We need to figure this out pronto."

Gregor, Jake, Ethan and Avery left.

He turned to Evangeline.

"You've been very quiet."

"I don't really have anything to say. All of this is out of my league. War and spies. I'm a sorcerer. I guard people, individuals mostly. I've never been involved in a war."

"You must have an opinion."

"I think you're right. Find the spy or spies first. Then decide what to do. If the spy's high enough in Roosevelt's organization, they need to be taken care of immediately. We want no whiff of anything leaking out to Collins."

"You have no opinion about going to war?"

"No. I'm not thrilled about it, but I also want revenge. Don't you?"

Damon stood and walked over to the beverage cart and poured another glass of water. Then drank it, feeling the cool liquid slide down his throat to an empty belly. He needed to remember to eat these days.

"I don't want revenge. My entire life here in the Zoo, I've watched revenge killing after revenge killing. Nothing was solved. The killer never felt better. Not really, not deeply enough. The person they were seeking revenge for was still gone. And a whole new cycle of revenge had just begun. That went on for decades. Until Morrigu and Roosevelt made peace with each other. I don't think killing Collins, or his loved ones, unless we somehow manage to kill everyone in their territory, will solve anything."

"You might be right. We must be sure to kill them all."

"Do you know how many people live in his territory? Our intel figured it was close to 50,000. And not like the scattered, impoverished villagers living off the land over here. His people are wealthy. Many have their own planes and their own armies, depending on Collins for further protection against hoodlums like us. They have tech we haven't even dreamed about. They know what type of equipment Collins has and they'll have bomb shelters and fenced compounds for protection against him. Just in case things go sour. The Eastside is nothing like here."

Damon was furious. He didn't want any of this. It was a foolish move. Didn't anyone else see this? They didn't have enough people or enough arms to take on Collins.

"I see your point, but I don't think you'll convince Morrigu. She is a war goddess after all."

"No, I don't suppose I will be able to convince her."

"So what are you going to do?" asked Evangeline.

"What I always do. Follow orders. Except this time, I doubt I'll come out alive."

"You might be surprised."

"I might. It happens occasionally. I don't suppose there's any sorcery you could do to help find that spy."

"I've been working on that. Seeing into people's minds and hearts. Haven't found one yet. It gives me a headache, that type of work, but I'll go back to it this afternoon."

"Good. Well, I better go see how they're getting on with the arms inventory. Suddenly, I'm in charge of Roosevelt's people as well as Morrigu's and I don't know anyone well enough to know who to promote."

"Good luck with that." Evangeline laughed, a clear, deep sound.

Damon left the warehouse, walking briskly. He needed to clear his head and reset his priorities. Or else he'd get himself killed.

He felt torn between what he should do and what he wanted. He wanted to leave. To run as far away from here as possible and escape this mess. He should stay and do what he was told.

Otherwise Morrigu would hunt him down herself, and kill him. She'd done it before, to his predecessor. It had been ugly and bloody. She'd made an example of the man. Torturing him publicly for days before finally killing him. He knew she wouldn't hesitate to do the same to him.

Damon made a circle around one group of warehouses. People looked busy when he saw them. Even before *they* saw him. There was a sense of urgency now. Things were afoot even if they didn't know what they were.

He was about to head to the near empty warehouse where any found arms were being taken when his wristband pinged.

"Damon. I need to talk to you."

Morrigu.

"Where are you?" he asked.

"Conference room."

"Be there in a few minutes."

He headed for the Castle. He dreaded having this conversation. Again.

When he arrived, Morrigu sat in an overstuffed chair, eating raspberries from a bowl and licking her red-tinged fingers. She motioned for Damon to sit down.

He sat back into the cushioned chair. This room was small. Insulated so no one could listen in through the walls. It was where Morrigu went to talk about private deals. No windows just like most of the Castle, it was lit by table and floor lamps. The lightbulbs were made by a small company in eastern Oregon and flown in, like most all the luxuries Morrigu and Roosevelt had. Luxuries he'd grown accustomed to over the years.

Morrigu drank some water, cleared her throat and said, "I understand you're not enthusiastic about this war."

"I am not. I've given you several reasons." He could feel her searching his mind and heart. Just as he would have when questioning a possible traitor, if he had the skill. There was no escaping her, she'd find out what she wanted, so he opened up. Knowing it could mean his death.

"But it's more than those, isn't it?"

"Yes. I'm tired. Humans don't live as long as deities. And those of us without magic live smaller lives, but no less passionate. I'm aging. I'm tired of fighting and I can't do it as well as I used to. I've been doing it my entire life. I just want to live. Simply and quietly."

"And yet you're good at fighting."

"I'm not good at the kind of fighting this war would entail. I can't fight against hundreds of people, hour after hour, hand to hand combat. And I don't understand the battle strategies using bombs, aircraft guns and automatic weapons. I understand street fighting. This is an entirely different kind of war. I'm afraid I'll botch things up."

"Afraid? That's a word I've never heard you use before."

"Yes afraid. I've always known my limits. That's why I'm so competent at so many things. And what you're asking of me is way beyond my limitations. And since I'm aging, I'm not as flexible as I once was. None of that is helped by the fact that we don't have enough arms or people to win this war."

"We only need one good person, one assassin to kill Collins."

"And then his son, or daughter, or brother or someone will take over and fly over here and obliterate us."

"There is that," said Morrigu, nodding her head in concession.

"I can't see a way to win here."

"So we should just keep on, life as usual. As if nothing had happened. As if they hadn't killed Young Roosevelt and many of our people. And injured Roosevelt so badly that it's possible he might never recover?"

"I don't know. I don't have answers, but I think we should explore other options. Not just leap towards revenge."

"I will consider what you have said. You have been my advisor longer than any other human. You have always helped me immensely."

"Thank you," said Damon, standing, sensing a dismissal.

"If I decide to go to war, and if I find someone with a better grasp of the battle strategies which you lack, what would you do?"

"What do you mean, what would I do?"

"I obviously can't keep you around here. You would have failed me. So what should I do with you?"

"Let me go." He shrugged.

"Let you go do what?"

"Let me leave. A long time ago, before the world was destroyed, people retired. They left their jobs, their work, and went off to create an entirely different life."

"Where would you go?"

"I don't know. I think I'd go off and live by myself. Hunt and fish to eat. Just be."

"You wouldn't go to Collins?"

"Out of the frying pan and into the fire? Hell no. And even if I wanted to, he wouldn't be stupid enough to take me. No, I'd choose a much different life than this. A peaceful one."

"You've grown soft," she said.

"Have I? Perhaps I have. I've enjoyed these years of peace between you and Roosevelt. Enjoyed learning about buying and selling jewelry and art. Enjoyed managing your empire and doing my part to keep you and everyone else safe."

"And you've been very good at it. I will think on this. And if I find someone, or you find someone to replace you, I might just let you go. Your heart isn't in a war, I can see that. Which compromises you. You know it and I know it. But, please tone it down during the meetings. It wouldn't be good if everyone knew. And you will tell no one about this conversation."

"I understand."

"I've got some paintings and jewelry to sell today. No matter what happens, we need to buy more planes and weapons. Send for Xavier and continue what you were doing."

Damon bowed and left the room. He called Xavier on his wristband and headed for the new arms warehouse.

Not really believing she'd let him go. Morrigu never let anyone go.

12

EVANGELINE

Evangeline walked through Morrigu's Blue Warehouse, listening in on people's thoughts. It was unpleasant. There was so much pain here. Hundreds of people had been badly burned. She didn't sense a spy among any of them.

Beds had been brought in now, from the rooms where people lived. Crisp white linens on all of them. Medical people in white jackets walked at the foot of the beds, fixing this or talking to that patient. Not enough medical people in this sea of white.

The smell was horrible. Even with the air circulation system. It had been able to keep out the smoke on the day of the attack and the time following, but it could do nothing with the stench of burned, rotting flesh.

Every now and then one of the patients screamed. Whether in terror or pain, Evangeline couldn't tell. One of the medical people would go and adjust the drip for their meds.

Roosevelt was sleeping, his head still bandaged along with

the rest of his body. She couldn't look at him. It hurt to see him lying there, in such pain, even with the drugs.

Collins' spy might be dead. They might not have known the attack was coming. It would have been risky for Collins to tell them. The spy might have acted differently. Even left the Zoo and been caught. Or they might have told someone. If they were dead, then Evangeline would never find them.

Evangeline walked out the door, into clean, fresh salt air coming off Puget Sound. She stood and breathed until the stench was out of her lungs. Then walked out towards the runway, where people were chipping away at cracked asphalt in preparation to rebuilding the runway.

She'd thoroughly checked out all of Roosevelt's household staff and bodyguards. None of them were Collins' spy. She was fairly sure about Jack, Ethan and Avery, although if one of them was a spy, they were probably highly skilled at hiding it. She was still watching them. None of them had given anything away during the meeting that morning. She'd been searching their minds at the same time Morrigu was, so she patterned her search efforts after Morrigu, in order to disguise herself from them. No use the three of them knowing she had that skill.

Evangeline chatted with the people working on the runway and was sure of them by the time she left. Her head ached. She decided to go back to her room and lie in the darkness.

Her room was in Roosevelt's living quarters, which was sadly empty. The bodyguards were either in the Blue Warehouse watching over Roosevelt and being unobtrusive, or taking turns salvaging things from the collapsed warehouse.

Roosevelt had made his living quarters modeled after a home. There was a living room, a kitchen to eat in, a formal dining room, bedrooms.

Evangeline had a bedroom two doors down from his. She unlocked and opened her door, walked in, switching overhead lights on, then closed it, locking it behind her. It was a square room, painted all blue, except for a golden circle on the ceiling, celebrating Lisa. There was a white moon in the tiles on the floor, in honor of Mawu, Lisa's twin and lover. Roosevelt had the room created for her. Evangeline had felt surprised, honored and embarrassed all at once.

This part of the world didn't understand her beliefs, so she'd planned on being very closed about them. Being a sorceress was strange enough. Leave it to Roosevelt to squash that plan.

Evangeline poured water from a pitcher and drank. Clean fresh water. She sat on the large bed covered with the soft, blue bedspread, untied her black boots and slipped them off. Then the socks. Once barefoot, she got up and walked across the cool tiles, stretching her feet, her toes. She walked into the tiny bathroom, still such a luxury. After she removed her clothes, she showered quickly and toweled off. She rolled her head around in a circle, stretching her neck.

Then the building rocked. The lights went off. Evangeline heard a large, deafening boom. She scrambled for her weapons. Switched the light of her wristband on. Quickly dressed and pulled on a pair of boots. Then ran out of her room.

Near the main entrance, the domestics were crowded around.

"What happened?" she asked.

"We don't know. We think it's another bomb."

Evangeline ran outside. Three planes circled. A pillar of smoke rose from the far end of the Zoo. One of the planes made another run at the buildings.

"Everybody out. Run for the trees!" Evangeline yelled.

She raced across the road to the fence and yanked open the spot that hadn't been repaired. The domestics and a couple of guards followed. She held it open until everyone was through and then went through herself.

Everyone was talking as they clumped beneath the trees.

"Silence," she whispered with a hiss.

She motioned to the guards to be looking out into the woods beyond. They were filled with bushes and brambles, but there was no guarantee Collins didn't have men on the ground.

There was another loud explosion and more smoke. She could see the flames now. Two of Morrigu's warehouses were gone. Evangeline wasn't sure whether to hope the Blue warehouse was one or not. Would it be better if all those people, including Roosevelt, were put out of their pain or if they lived?

The third plane came through and dropped a bomb that leveled the warehouse Evangeline had just left. Destroying her room, all of Roosevelt's precious collections and all the food for Roosevelt's people.

Then the planes roared one after the other making a run above all the buildings and shooting guns. Killing anyone outside the warehouses. The planes rose and circled above the Zoo, before they flew upwards and off to the east. Out of sight.

Smoke filled the Zoo. There was no wind today. Evangeline tore the bottom off her shirt and tied it over her face, motioning for the others to do the same.

"Let's go find the survivors," said Evangeline.

As they walked through the Zoo, there were only two warehouses left standing. One held the arms rescued from the first attack. The other housed many of Morrigu's people.

The Blue Warehouse was gone. Roosevelt was gone. All the medical people and supplies gone.

Everyone gathered in the arms warehouse, which was empty except for a small corner that contained crates of weapons and ammunition.

Evangeline tried to get a head count. Maybe a hundred people. Far too few for an army. Were there others outside? People who hadn't come in? People who were helping the wounded?

Morrigu was there, Damon was too.

Damon quieted everyone and said, "We don't know if they'll be back. We have to assume they will. For some reason, they only bought three planes again this time. The bombs were larger though. We have no planes now. Which means we're out of business. We can't buy and sell jewelry, art, alcohol or gas and oil. We've got nothing except ourselves. We have to leave or we'll lose that."

Morrigu nodded, her rage apparent.

"We have nowhere to go," said Damon.

Morrigu said, "We will go to the village. Where those people were from. They will take us in."

Evangeline watched as Damon's face flashed a look of shock, before he recovered and showed no emotion.

"I don't know the way," he said. "I was concentrating on dynamics inside the van, not on traveling."

Eamon stepped forward and said, "I remember how to get there. I was driving. Although we'll be walking. It will be a long walk. If we've got injured, then at least two long days. If we run into trouble, and some of those areas were dicey, it'll take longer."

"Do we have enough weapons to arm everyone?" asked Morrigu.

Damon looked around and said, "Enough to arm those who want to carry a weapon. Not everyone though."

"Good. We will spend the rest of the afternoon salvaging and packing. Anything that can't be carried will be left behind. We have few medical supplies. Anyone who's badly injured, unable to walk unassisted, will be killed. All bodies will be put on the burning warehouses. They will be our funeral pyres," said Morrigu.

"Our wristbands don't work anymore, not since Roosevelt's and Morrigu's homes went down, taking all our tech with it. Anything electric or any tech will be destroyed. Make sure everyone brings nothing like that with us. We'll collect your wristbands as you leave here."

People looked shocked. Many of them had never been without a wristband, not since they were very young. Always in touch with the network. Able to talk to others from a distance.

Why were they collecting them though? And why all electrics? The villagers had electrics. To make everyone's load lighter?

No, she decided. It was to make everyone oversee the others. To make sure if the spy was still alive and with them, that Collins couldn't track them. That no spy had any means of communicating with him.

Evangeline sighed. She had nothing to pack. Everything that she wasn't wearing had been destroyed. Thank goodness she'd gotten some clothes, boots and weapons. Too bad about all her other beautiful clothes.

What was she thinking? Hundreds of people were dead and she was mourning clothes. She shook her head, trying to regain focus.

Damon was going around putting people in charge of things. Finding food to pack. Finding other supplies.

"Those of you in Morrigu's housing, your home is still standing. I'm afraid you'll have to share with Roosevelt's people who've lost everything except what they're wearing. Our first priorities are: food, water, clothing, medical supplies and weapons. Survival items. Anything else must be left behind. Go gather up your things. Those of you with no things to collect, we will search for those items. Move over to the right side of the warehouse and I'll organize you. We will have a small meal tonight once all the food is gathered and split up. Followed by a funeral service for our dead. Tonight is the last night any of us will be sleeping inside. Let's get moving, there's a lot to do. We leave as soon as it's light tomorrow."

Damon moved to the right side of the warehouse and waited for people to gather there. He assigned some of them to help gather food. Others to search for any medical supplies or weapons.

The rest, mostly Roosevelt's guards and Evangeline, he said, "You'll help me search for bodies and for people who are severely wounded. Those who are too injured to walk, we must kill quickly. Save your bullets, use knives. I'm sorry, but there's no other way. Anyone unable to do that, collect bodies. We'll be piling them on the burning Blue Warehouse. Team up and get moving."

As they left the warehouse, two people stood on each side of the door, collecting wristbands. Evangeline tossed hers in the metal bin.

Damon went out last, tossing his in.

"Take these to Carlos. He'll deactivate them."

He made sure the two guards had put their wristbands in. The two men hauled off the metal bin.

Evangeline covered her face with the torn shirt mask again and set out with Kahlil. They found two people badly burned and each killed one. Then made trips to take the bodies to the fire.

She told herself it was a mercy killing. No medical supplies or people to help them. Even though she was right, it didn't make those deaths easier.

Mostly, they collected dead bodies and hauled them to the pyres. There were no tractors or functioning machinery anymore. They'd all been destroyed in the bombings. Everything had to be done with human muscles.

By the time they'd finished both she and Kahlil were covered with blood. They went towards Morrigu's housing and Damon found them.

"We've got one generator running. Enough to pump some water. Get in there and get a shower before the gasoline runs out. Then line up and eat."

Evangeline was not going to eat tonight. She'd smelled too much burned flesh to last a lifetime.

After the quick shower, Evangeline was given fresh clothes. She'd washed her bloody clothes in the shower, and wrung them out, carrying them with her. She cleaned her boots off as best she could. Some of those blood stains would never come out. But they were well made boots and it would probably be a long time before she was able to get better ones. Who knew what sort of wilderness they were heading out into?

She drank water while the others ate. The smell of food nauseated her. It was all she could do to keep down the water.

After dinner everyone moved off to what had been the Blue Warehouse. The place was still burning hot and smelled of smoke and roasting meat.

Morrigu stood in front of the burning pyre, wearing a black gown trimmed with red accents, her hair flowing loose and wild. She did indeed look like a goddess of war and death. Her voice deep and vibrant as if she was gaining power from the release of souls.

"Our brothers, sisters, daughters, sons and friends, we give up to the fire. May they find the peace they need. Their souls free now, to wander where they will. Their flesh and bones will return to the earth who gave them life. Their burdens gone. Let us remember their heroism and power and forget their weaknesses. We will take their memories and their history with us as we travel to a new home and they will live on. Some of their souls may choose to guard this place. To keep others away, serving as a warning. Give thanks for their lives and their presence in our lives."

Then she began to speak in a language Evangeline didn't recognize. It was hypnotic all the same. No one else around her seemed to recognize it either, although they seemed to be almost in a trance. The language was lilting and guttural at the same time. Full of drama and softness. Morrigu's speaking became chanting which transformed into singing.

Colored lights swirled in the smoke. They took shapes of deities and animals moving around each other, as if in a dance. The air felt charged with magic. It wasn't all Morrigu's. Those deities were here, drawn by death and sorrow. Many in the crowd were openly weeping. This seemed to go on for hours. Evangeline spotted Kalfu in the smoke. Roosevelt was on his arm and they were both smoking cigars and laughing.

Morrigu finished in their language again. "Go in peace. Find some sleep. Rest and be easy."

Evangeline felt exhausted. She followed everyone else into the housing for Morrigu's people. Someone gave her a blanket and she found a couch in one of the common rooms. She was asleep within minutes.

Tomorrow would be a hard day.

13

CADY

It was moving day. Bright and sunny as soon as the sun crested the trees. By then, Cady had packed her few belongings. Bedding, clothes, a few herb roots, some seeds and her food. Plus two books. One, a field guide to native plants. The other, a guide to garden plants. Both might come in handy. She'd decided to wear her weapons. It wouldn't do any good having them in a bag if the villagers were attacked.

She packed her two bags of belongings into the box Joe had attached to the back of the bike. It was a bit ungainly, but easier than carrying them. She tied them to the wire box so nothing would bounce off. Then tied on her four ancient, stainless steel water bottles, freshly filled. Then went back and closed her door, patting the house.

"Thank you for giving me shelter. I appreciated it."

Onyx sat watching her, waiting to leave. Everyone in the village had met him and approved him as an addition to their moving party.

Then she picked up Monster, who knew something strange was going on. She put the harness and leash on him.

"C'mon dear, you'll need to wear this today. Just in case something happens, I might need you to move quickly. Let's put you in your own space. I'm not leaving you behind."

He purred as she put him into the pet box on the bike with his new special blanket, that probably smelled like her. She'd gotten him used to sleeping in the box for the last two weeks. And she'd even gotten him used to wearing the harness and leash. He was an amazingly adaptable cat for being an adult, Sharine had told her.

The pet box was snugly attached, just in front of the handlebar, so Cady could keep an eye on him and talk to him. Monster curled up, ready to sleep.

She wheeled the bike towards the village, shifting her rifle, so it hung just right and was easy to get to. The others were mostly ready and they moved off, following Onyx and Gia, who was leading them. Onyx's bulk flattened the foliage, creating a trail which made it easier for them all to move through the underbrush. Being at the front kept Onyx well away from the livestock, who were still quite afraid of the dragon.

As the day wore on, they traveled through forest, then heavy brush. Tall Douglas firs grew out of the ruins of old houses. They passed over buckled streets filled with alder clumps. Thorny blackberries grew everywhere.

Cady had read in one of her books that the blackberries had been brought to this country from Armenia, wherever that was, for their fruit. They had become an invasive weed and taken over.

Onyx's hard scales broke ground for them. The dragon's chest tore through the blackberries without a thought and the bulk of its body made a wide enough trail for even the carts. Its dragging tail creating a rut which made it easy for Cady to wheel her bike through. Onyx was following a path already used by feral goats, coyotes, wild dogs and who knows what else. Cady had seen an occasional herd of deer by Greenlake, but they were far and few between. Hunted relentlessly for their meat by those with no care or thought about anyone's future food source.

The day grew hotter and hotter. Sweat rolled down her face and body. She covered Monster's carrier with a cloth, hoping to keep the hot sun off. They stopped for a time beneath some large trees. To rest and eat. Those carrying children, or herding them, really needed the rest.

Cady let Monster out of his carrier, giving him some water in the palm of her hand, which he drank happily. He wandered as far as the leash would let him, looking warily at two boys who chased each other around. Then sat next to Cady, eating pieces of dried goat meat which she gave him. She chewed on the dried meat, too. Ate a carrot from her garden. The crunchy carrot tasted sweet and strong, with an earthy flavor. The goat meat, well drying was the only way to preserve it. It had been better fresh. But it was food.

Their party spread out for quite a length, with all the people and animals. Sheep, llamas, goats, a few horses which were mostly being ridden. Dogs running back and forth, most of them helping herd the other animals. Chickens and other birds were caged and riding in small carts being pulled by heavy horses who were led.

Sarah and Beth's kids had brought along some kittens, in small carts they took turns pulling. The mother had been feral and wouldn't have anything to do with people. But they'd gotten the kittens after weaning, but early enough to be able to make friends with them. The kittens were in pet boxes, stuck in the boxes until the destination was reached.

After the rest, the villagers moved onwards. Several people at the tail end of the train were fluffing up the broken and battered foliage, trying to obliterate the trail of their passage.

Cady didn't see how that was going to work, but she hoped things would grow back to normal before anyone came looking for the village. If anyone did, which was unlikely.

The smell was different now, dusty. They'd passed from the trees onto a wide plain. Dried grasses and weeds. There was no water here and it was blindingly hot.

They crested a hill and on the other side saw a valley of crumbled, burnt ruins, filled with more dried grasses and weeds, plus a few green bushes. Several charred trees stood sentinel, the tallest structures. A fire had swept through, perhaps last year. Now nature was reclaiming it.

The short plants would grow first, followed by bushes. Then trees would move in and it would become forest, until the cycle began again. Might take hundreds of years, she'd read. Or, in the case of calamity like fire or quake, might happen any time. Her books and observation had taught Cady marvelous things.

Halfway up the hill across the valley, the forest began again. That was the where the fire had burned out. Mostly deciduous trees. She could spot the alder with its grayish bark and big leaf maple. A few evergreen madronas near the edge of the fire line, identifiable by their reddish, peeling bark and open structure.

Gia said, "We go over that ridge and down there is our lake, I think."

The sun was setting off to their left. Sunlight had been waning for quite a while, but Cady hadn't noticed. The heat hadn't gone down though.

"Do we stop, or keep going until we make it?" Gia asked.

Mazzy said, "I don't like stopping in such an open spot."

Sam wiped his face with his hands and said, "I'm exhausted. So are all the kids. But it'll be cooler to travel by night. If we can just rest a bit and eat. Then we can go on."

Cady was exhausted too. She hadn't walked so much in years. And her still healing thigh throbbed with pain. She let Monster out of his box, then plopped down onto the ground, but not before grabbing a water bottle and food.

He was so hot, he panted. She gave him more water then wiped her hands on his head, wetting his fur. Maybe it would cool him somewhat. The water was still cold in her bottles. They were heavy and insulated and she felt the cool water slide down her throat. She was grateful for the moisture.

Onyx took off flying. Probably to look ahead, or possibly to stretch. The dragon's dark wings were silhouetted against the deep blue of the sky.

Cady ate and fed Monster. Then she must have dozed off. She was woken by activity as everyone around her got up and packed their belongings again.

Monster was gazing intently at a small lizard that scuttled past. He leapt and caught it, seemingly knowing exactly where the leash ended. Then ate it.

Cady stood, putting the food and water away. She interrupted Monster's post meal bath to put him back in the box. She removed the cloth from on top of it. The air would flow better and hopefully everything would cool now that the sun was down.

Onyx returned with the moonrise, luckily it was full and would light their way for a time. Sam walked beside him now. They picked their way down into the valley and across it. The roads were sometimes usable for a short way. Buckled by the quake, obscured by fallen trees or even buildings in other places. It took a long time to make their way through the rubble. Clearing the road sometimes meant four men taking axes to the trees trunks. Which took awhile. Onyx helped, lifting away as much as the dragon could fly away with.

The moon passed to its highest point as they began to climb upwards again. Cady figured they must be getting closer. The group was quiet now. Not enough energy to talk. The children mostly asleep. Those that were awake seemed cranky, but mostly quiet.

They group paused just after they made it inside the forest. To rest a bit. They still had to reach the top of the ridge, but everyone needed a break.

Sharine came past and asked, "How's your leg? I noticed you were limping."

"It hurts."

"Here's some salve you can rub on it," she said, handing Cady a tin. "It might help the pain some. Use it now and then when we stop for good." Sharine moved on to check on someone else. Did the woman never rest?

There was no privacy here, but everyone was minding their own. Cady dropped her pants, rubbed the salve on her thigh and pulled them back up.

Monster meowed plaintively.

"Yes, yes, I'll let you out."

She did and gave him more water after he'd dug a hole, done his business and covered it. Cady ate more carrots. And a piece of goat cheese which she shared with Monster.

"We're getting closer. Soon, we'll be in our new home. With whatever that brings."

He purred and sat on her lap, watching the other villagers intently.

Then it was time for one last push. Onyx said their new

village was over the hill and down towards the lake. The dragon hadn't landed down there. Hadn't wanted to alarm those who'd gone ahead and didn't know about the dragon. But Onyx had seen and smelled a fire and humans.

Cady's leg felt a bit better as they continued on up the hill. It wasn't a thick forest, so Onyx and Sam were able to find a path wide enough, removing bushes and saplings as they went. It was slow going though.

The smell was refreshing after the dust of the fire-burned valley and the air was cooler among all the trees. As they crested the hill, more evergreen trees sprung up around them. Tall Douglas firs and Hemlocks with their soft needles. In a clearing, a clump of huckleberries was found and people stopped, to pick and eat the sweet, dark berries.

They began going downhill, although there was no view. The forest was thick here. It was rough moving between the tall bushes. And the foliage let little moonlight in. There were a couple of flashlights in the group, but people were saving them for emergencies. Onyx could see and everyone else closely followed whoever was in front of them. The only sound was the snapping of branches as people and horses stepped on them. The other animals had smaller hooves and made less noise.

The hill became steep enough that Sam and Onyx made a trail that cut across the hill gradually going down, then walked back the other direction still going downhill. They did this twice. It made the trip longer, but Cady didn't feel like she'd lose control of her bike. The bike felt very heavy. Her legs and arms were becoming shaky. They'd been going for hours upon hours. She couldn't imagine what those with heavy carts were going through.

Then the ground leveled off and they came out of the

forest. There were still a few trees, but the land was more open with bushes and grasses. Cady could see the lake and smell the moisture. Down below, near the shore, she saw a cluster of houses, not quite on the shore. Up from it a ways. Enough to account for any spring flooding of the lake.

There was no one about. The moon was close to setting over the far horizon and the sun wasn't up yet. A streak of moonlight grazed the calm surface of the lake, making it look like paradise.

Sam said, "This is our new home. They've built a lot since we found the place."

A slight breeze blew past and Cady could feel the sweat on her body. The lake looked like a good place for a swim.

Sam said, "There's a creek that runs down that hill, just on the other side of the village. It's fresh and clean. That's where we'll get our water until a well is dug." He pointed to the far side of the houses.

They crossed over to a large fenced area and Sam told the herders to put all their animals in. The fencing had been scheduled as the first project. A stout wooden fence, with wire to keep the goats in, when they weren't grazing elsewhere.

Cady watched as the goats, sheep and llamas filed in. Happy to be allowed to just rest and eat fresh grass.

There were full troughs, the water shining in the moonlight. Cady could see a pipe emptying into the first trough, which overflowed into the second and so on. Fresh water poured through the troughs and then another pipe came out of the lowest trough leading down towards an area near the edge of the lake, filled with cattails and iris.

The sun began to peek over the hillside to the east, casting long shadows from the tall wide trees. Cady didn't recognize what kind they were.

By the time all the animals were all inside the fence, and the horses unsaddled, Bao and Will had appeared, wary at the sight of the dragon.

Onyx had lain down and curled up like a cat. Pretending to sleep, although Cady saw the dragon had one eye open. Just in case the new humans needed watching.

Mazzy and Gia were explaining the dragon situation to the two men who looked unconvinced. It wasn't long before Tank, Joaquin, Ryan, Brady and Mateo came out of the houses. Joaquin ran to his family, as did Brady and Mateo. The others talked to their friends, while looking warily at Onyx, who had closed its eyes and was asleep.

The sun was up now. Chickens and other birds was been released from their cages, been fed dried corn and seeds. They began scavenging for bugs.

Tank found Cady and said, "I'll take you to your house if you want."

"I have my own house?"

"Yes. We built it a bit apart from the others. Knew you liked your privacy."

"I'd love to see it. I don't know if I can stand for much longer."

"Take my arm then." He took the handlebars of her bike and wheeled it off, as she took his arm. She leaned a lot of her weight on him. Good thing he was such a big man.

On the way to her house, Tank pointed out the outhouse they'd dug.

"That's the closest one to your house."

She stopped to make use of it.

Her house was across the stream, over a large wooden bridge and in a forested area. Down below that was a meadow where she could plant her garden.

The little house was made of newly cut logs and smelled like fir. It was a welcoming, grounding scent. Several large windows let in the light. There were little hooks on each side to hang cloth over the windows. It had a metal door with a screen in it to keep insects out and a wooden door that closed over that, both from the old times. She'd never seen such a thing.

It was a bit larger than her old house. The men had salvaged an old wood stove and it sat on a brick area in the center of the room. There was a pile of already chopped wood nearby. The men had also made her a table, two chairs and a platform for a bed. There was a counter against one wall with a metal sink in it.

"The drain goes to a pipe that takes it out to the forest. So you can fill the sink with hot water to wash things, then pull up this plug and the soapy water goes out to water some bushes. You can even move the end of the pipe if you think it's too much for the bushes."

"Amazing," she said.

There was a cat flap in the wall up near one of the windows that led to a shelf on the wall. On the outside was also a wood shelf.

"Hopefully, that way raccoons or other critters won't find it easily, but the cat will. Oh, and beneath the house, you access it from the outside, is a root cellar. We're all going to need them."

"This is wonderful. Thank you so much. I didn't expect anything like this."

"We appreciate everything you've done for us. Going back into the Zoo was a brave thing. We'll make sure you're taken care of."

"Well, thank you. I think I'll get some rest."

"Do you need any help unpacking?" he asked.

"No. I'll just let Monster out. The rest can wait."

Tank nodded and left.

Cady wheeled her bike inside the house and closed the metal door, then noticed that it locked from the inside. So she locked it, smiling. She'd never had a door that locked before. The breeze flowing in through the screen was welcome. She got the pet carrier and set it on the floor, letting Monster out. Then took off the harness and leash.

He prowled around for a bit, meowing. She gave him fresh cool water and some dried goat meat, then drank a sip of the still cold water. It tasted clean and refreshing. She hoped the water around here was as good.

Monster ate and drank, but kept moving around. Restless. She put his blanket up on the shelf and put him up there, showing him the cat flap. And he was gone, out exploring.

Cady unrolled her blankets on the bed platform and set down her pillow. She took off her boots and socks. The wood floor felt cool and smooth beneath her feet. Someone had done a good job sanding it. Sunlight shone in through two of the windows and she found cloth to hang over the hooks to cut the light a bit. Not that she couldn't sleep in daylight.

The third window was on the north side of the house and wasn't as much of a problem. She'd deal with it later. All the windows had metal screening on the other side of the glass. She opened the north window and a cool fragrant breeze from the forest blew through. She smiled. This house came with everything. She could leave the windows open and bugs would stay outside.

She took her filthy clothes off and changed into fresher ones, then lay down on the hard wood platform. Swimming to clean up could wait till after sleeping. She'd miss her feather bed though. Tomorrow she would go looking for dried grasses to stuff her now empty mattress with. She'd considered bringing it filled with all the feathers, but that would have been too bulky.

Cady fell asleep even before the next thought. Dreaming about a new life.

14

DAMON

Damon woke abruptly. He'd fallen asleep sitting up in a chair and his back hurt. Hell, everything hurt. He was sitting in the common eating area of Morrigu's workers' housing. The cooks had just began making their last meal there. It wouldn't be hot, there was no electricity.

Generators were out. Gasoline almost all used up. There was a bit left that would be used in two of the three vans they'd bring with them, to carry the weapons and heavy equipment. The third van was electric and fully charged. Wouldn't last long, but they'd use it as long as they could.

Damon stood and stretched, trying to loosen his stiff muscles. He hadn't slept long, maybe an hour or two, but it had to be enough.

What a nightmare this was. Leading all these people, descending on that poor village and taking it by force if necessary. It was a mistake. Morrigu expected to be welcomed. Well, they wouldn't be. They might have to fight. The village was armed. Prosperous enough for that. But they probably didn't have enough food to feed double their population. And winter was coming on.

Morrigu's people would never make it otherwise. Not most of them. They didn't know how to grow food. And if they wanted warmth and any sort of electricity, they'd have to re-engineer all their tech to work on solar or wind. Damon had no idea if there was anyone at the Zoo still alive who had the knowledge or skill to do that.

He rubbed his face. It was covered with stubble, but there'd be no more shaving for him. Damon walked over to the counter where a pitcher of water sat near empty glasses. He poured a glass of water and drank the entire thing. It was cold and tasted flat and flavorless. Water too would become something they'd have to think about. Surely the village had clean water. Was it lake water? Or was there a nearby creek that was clean? Or a well?

Late into the night, Morrigu and he had talked. Rather, she'd paced around the room and he'd tried to work out other solutions than descending on the village without warning.

Morrigu had been thinking and Damon felt sure it wasn't about how they'd survive till spring. She was thinking about revenge. Still.

Damon grabbed a ripe apple from a metal bowl and a hunk of meat that had been roasted last night, in the coals from Morrigu's burned castle. The cooks had been scrambling to deal with perishable food and make it edible without using any electricity. He didn't envy their work.

The ham was delicious, juicy and moist. He finished eating it, just standing there and licked his fingers. Wiping them on his smokey-smelling pants. Everything he owned, which hadn't been much, had been burned along with Morrigu's Castle and almost the rest of the Zoo. He hadn't taken any of the clean clothes, leaving them for others. He had taken a jacket though. It would be getting cold during the nights soon and he had no confidence they'd be living indoors any time soon.

It was getting light outside and people were filing into the room to find food.

Damon left and walked outside. It was still smokey. He headed towards where people had put together packs for everyone to carry. There was a line of people already formed. Waiting to leave. Their faces grim.

He got four water bottles from one line. Two of them were flimsy plastic, the others stainless steel. He'd use up the plastic ones first. Minimize the leaching of nasty chemicals into his water. He clipped those to his belt, with clips that lay in a pile nearby.

He chose one of the heavier packs, putting the other water bottles inside it. Took off the jacket, rolled it up and stuffed it inside. Then shouldered the pack. It would work, but he'd be tired at the end of the day.

Then Damon moved down the line to where Gregor was handing out weapons. He'd assigned Gregor the task, knowing the man would be able to do the job. Most of the people he'd assigned to jobs Damon didn't feel the same confidence about.

Gregor stood near the electric vans. Three of them were still running and would carry the heavy stuff for the community. Mostly weapons and arms. One held the tech equipment Carlos was able to salvage at the last minute, at least two functioning computers and other components. They had lots of information on them, but there'd be no way to hook into any network where they were headed.

Gregor nodded at him and handed Damon a couple of belts of ammo and a large rifle. Damon automatically checked if the rifle was loaded, even though he could already see the magazine in it. He was tired. Too tired.

"Do you have enough ammo for your handgun?"

"No, I'll take some."

Gregor pointed Damon to the row of open plastic bins. Damon found the right size and put three cases in his pack. Then put the pack on, the belts on and slung the rifle strap over the top of it all, arranging it for easy access. If they were attacked out on the trail, there would be no warning.

Gregor went back to talking to people about what they could handle as a weapon. Many people didn't want a weapon.

Damon looked at the other bins. Some of them were full of handguns and knives.

He took a big knife and strapped it on. Not for fighting, that wasn't his weapon, but for living outdoors. It was a shame to use a fine knife for cutting kindling or skinning game, but there it was. They were reduced to that.

The last stop was a pile of clothes. Coats, hats, heavy boots. Damon took someone's old canvas hat. It was waterproof and had a wide brim all the way around. A bit warm for this weather, but he'd be glad of it when the rains came. And it would keep the hot sun off his head. His hair was thinning and he hadn't seen the sun this much in years. He didn't need a sunburn on top of exhaustion.

Then he stood in a clump with everyone else. The Zoo had once held a multitude of people. Now they were down to a couple hundred people. And he only counted twelve kids. All of the children of Roosevelt's people had been lost, along with most of their parents. So many people gone.

Things went faster than Damon anticipated they would and in no time, the group was off, following Morrigu and

Eamon, who was leading them because he remembered the way.

Morrigu was dressed in the same clothes as yesterday, all her belongings burnt too. A long green tunic of silky material, green pants and low-heeled boots. She too, wore a pack, a fairly heavy one from the looks of it. And a very long knife, as well as a bow with a quiver of arrows.

Damon worked his way to the edge of the middle of the crowd. People with guns had been instructed to stay to the edges and be guards, alert for trouble, but not firing, unless fired upon. The three vans, also heavily guarded, brought up the rear.

They left the Zoo by the front gate, he heard the clank as the gates closed and locked. Then they went up the street running next to the compound. They traveled north for a mile, maybe two. It felt like two. Walking down the wide, four lane road. Abandoned cars lined the edges. They were missing all the mechanical parts, those long ago salvaged and repurposed.

A couple miles north the group turned right onto a one lane road. It was still asphalt and it might once have been a wider road that was being reclaimed by trees and bushes. Some of the bushes were clumps of blackberries and people were picking and eating them as they walked.

Damon picked one, but it tasted tart. He spat it out.

"You need to pick the soft ones, those come off easily with your fingers," said a woman behind him. He recognized her as one of the cooks.

He tried again and found a soft one. The flavor was rich, intense and sweet. Definitely good.

As they moved farther away from the Zoo, the side streets became more ragged and overgrown. Nature had taken back what humans had stolen.

Side roads held downed trees and old rotten power poles that had fallen, dragging their wires with them. Most of the cables near the Zoo had long been taken and reused, but as they got farther out, scavenging seemed less common. Most of the houses had fallen, but some still stood, rotting away gracefully.

The sun rose in the sky and heat poured down on them. Damon was sweating from the exertion, but he didn't take the hat off, no matter how hot he was. He could smell that most of the people nearby were sweating too. None of them were used to carrying heavy loads for mile upon mile.

Surrounded by trees, bushes and tall plants, the only open space was the main road, kept in repair. Where the asphalt had cracked and buckled, someone had removed it, replacing it with gravel. Who was that someone?

At midday they stopped in the middle of the road to rest. Damon took off his rifle and pack. Put his rifle back on. He stretched and drank water. Ate a ham sandwich which had been put in his pack, savoring the succulent ham and tangy mustard.

Morrigu was walking through the crowd. Damon knew she had no actual need to eat, she just did it for pleasure. Her sustenance was from people following her and from the land. She stopped when she saw him.

"I wondered if you'd come."

"Did I have a choice?" he asked.

"Perhaps not. I know you like the villagers and are worried we will hurt them, although I admit, I don't understand how we could hurt them. We just want them to take us in. To give us a place to live and hide for a time. To allow us to find a new spot and rebuild."

"And what if we decide we like their village and we'll

rebuild there? What if they are pushed off their land or if we bring our war to them? They are not warriors. They're farmers and craftspeople. They can't survive a war."

She said, "We need farmers and craftspeople. We have very little food. They can teach our people how to find and grow food."

"Then we will become farmers and herders. Not warriors. Who will fight the war?" asked Damon.

"I don't know. I'm not convinced we need to fight a war to kill Collins. I have a plan, but it's not finished yet. I'm not ready to share it. Right now, I just need to make sure my people survive and thrive."

He nodded. He wanted that too. Just not at the expense of the villagers.

Morrigu moved on through the crowd. Damon later saw her talking to Evangeline, far back on the edge of the group. Evangeline looked tired and angry.

She sure hadn't signed up for this. She'd been hired by Roosevelt and had probably expected a life lived in luxury. Where they were heading wasn't going to be that.

They'd just gotten started again when they heard the planes.

"Take cover everyone! Under the trees!" yelled Damon.

He pushed people in front of him, under bushes and trees. The vans pulled as far underneath as they could, mostly hidden.

The planes flew overhead, en route to the Zoo.

It wasn't long before the bombs dropped again. One. Two. Three.

This time were was no artillery fire from the planes. There was no one running away to shoot at. At least there shouldn't be. If some fool had stayed behind. ...

Damon heard the planes bank and dive, probably searching for any survivors of the attack. Satisfied, they finally flew off. Heading back to the Eastside, he hoped. Reporting that everyone from the Zoo was finally all dead.

When he could no longer hear the planes, Damon signaled they should move on. The day had grown hot and the sun blasted down on the cleared road.

People were sobbing. For some of them, the Zoo was the only home they'd ever known. For him it held a few good memories, but mostly bad ones. During the time before Morrigu and then when she was first climbing to power, he'd lost a lot of friends. Until he learned to stop making friends. Those had been dark years and he wouldn't allow himself to feel that pain again. He hadn't made any friends since. Refused to let himself care about anyone.

They passed by a cleared area. Damon could see a house and fields that had been planted. Stout, short brick walls surrounded the fields and cattle grazed there. Dogs leapt up on top of the wall barking and baying at the group as they passed. Damon could see four men with guns in the shadows of the porch.

They kept walking.

There was another homestead they passed later. Wire fences keeping in goats, sheep and other animals Damon didn't recognize, but could smell. There were several houses and a large garden fenced in with wire. There were many more people with guns standing around. And several large aggressive dogs.

It wasn't until mid-afternoon that Eamon found the narrow, one lane, gravel road walled in by the hedge of blackberries and glossy-leaved bushes. It felt cooler in the shade of the tall hedge and their group stretched out into a line four to five people deep.

Damon motioned to the other guards and gradually moved up to the front. No one was going to be able to attack them from the side here. And the next break would be at the wide turnaround. After that the village.

He didn't want to have any part of this, but he'd long ago bound himself to Morrigu. For bad or worse, there was no going back now.

Soon, the first three rows behind Eamon and Morrigu were filled with guards. And Evangeline, who he guessed was a guard now too.

As they approached the gravel area, he saw no signs of the villagers. Morrigu stopped, allowing everyone to move into the open area. She looked at Damon.

"I have no idea what to expect," he said.

"I shall go in first and talk to them. Alone."

"I'll go too," said Evangeline.

"No," said Morrigu. "I must go alone."

Evangeline shrugged.

Damon knew better than to argue.

"I'll wait for your signal," he said.

Morrigu went down the trail Eamon pointed to alone. She disappeared behind a thick tree and obscuring bushes. There was too much noise coming from the crowd behind Damon to hear anything.

He turned and motioned to silence everyone. Even the vehicles shut off their engines. There was still no sound from the village. After a time, Morrigu reappeared.

"They are all gone. The village is deserted."

"What?" asked Damon.

He ran down the trail, followed by Evangeline. There was no sign of any people, or animals. A few small brown birds flitted through the towering trees. He checked several buildings as Evangeline checked others. Sometimes old furniture had been left, and a few scattered belongings like books or cracked cups. Crops had mostly been harvested, although there were a few shriveling vines left. It looked like they might need water.

There were no fires burning anywhere, those were long cold. He checked Cady's house last, puzzled by the tracks of a massive creature intermingled with her bootprints. Had some large beast chased the villagers away?

But her house looked clean and tidy. The mattress was there, but not the blankets or pillow she'd had on her bed. Books seemed to be missing from the bookcase. It smelled pleasantly of herbs, but there were none hanging to dry. It didn't look like she'd fled. Not suddenly anyway.

He went back to the center of the village, everyone had gathered there and was sitting down, resting. Damon took his rifle off, dropping his pack.

He took Eamon's arm, "Have the vehicles been hidden?"

"Yeah, I had them park under the trees. They're cutting branches to cover them."

"Good."

Damon stood there, watching the crowd. There was some cut firewood the villagers had left and the cooks began making a fire in a pit in the center of the abandoned village.

Someone else was walking between buildings and writing things down, as if taking a count of beds. Others were organizing a watch. Still others carrying buckets of water.

Where had the villagers gone? And when? They couldn't have been gone more than a week. The tracks around Cady's house were fresh. Not overrun by animals. And why had they left?

They had a seer. One who could see long term. Had they seen the remnants of the Zoo coming? Or was it something else?

People were assigned houses to stay in. There were more houses than people and some chose to sleep on the floor of already full buildings rather than be off alone in single room houses. They were afraid, wanting to cling to each other, he knew.

Damon wasn't assigned a house and Morrigu told him to choose an empty one. She didn't feel the need of a bodyguard out here in the woods. Not yet anyway.

He wandered through the village, listening as people made discoveries. Most of them had never lived in a house before, just in Morrigu's large warehouses, converted into apartments. These houses had windows that opened to let in fresh air. Some had large tubs to bathe in. And there were wood stoves to keep each of the houses warm during winter. The former villagers hadn't taken the cut firewood with them. They must have been traveling light. In a hurry to get somewhere or leave here.

Gregor found several handwritten books with diagrams in one of the houses. He brought them to Carlos, who had invented Morrigu's network that all the wristbands ran on. The older man sat at a table in the village center and pored over the books and made surprised grunting sounds. Then he'd hand them off to his daughter, Martina, who read them and also exclaimed.

"We can do this, can't we?" she asked.

"What?" asked Damon.

Martina said, "These books explain how the former

inhabitants made a solar and wind powered electrical system. They took the wiring with them, but we saw plenty more on our journey here. It would be easy to collect. We can have electricity by the time cold weather comes. That'll give us light and then we can rebuild our system."

"Great," said Damon. "I'll tell Morrigu, there's hope."

Carlos and Martina hadn't heard him, they were back to reading.

Damon ate with the others as the sky darkened. The cooks made vegetable stew out of what they harvested from the former villagers' gardens and what they'd brought along. It tasted spicy and was filling.

Like the others, Damon finished eating, washed his bowl and spoon in a bin of hot, soapy water, then rinsed it as instructed and left it in another bin to dry. Amazing what the cooks had been able to bring with them.

He wandered off in the near darkness, bringing his pack and guns with him. Finally, he found Cady's house and went inside. It was nice to be away from the others. To hear no one chattering away. His head felt full of voices. Everyone was still worried and he couldn't shake their worries.

Damon slept, waking periodically to strange shrieking noises of birds and other wild beasts. He had no light with him to investigate and was too tired to care. If something wanted to kill him, he was willing to let it. For tonight.

Tomorrow, he'd find a light.

15

EVANGELINE

Evangeline woke, stiff from lying on a lumpy straw mattress which sat on a wooden frame. She'd tossed and turned all night. Woken by bird screeches and a vaguely familiar hissing-coughing noise.

Once, during the night, she'd gotten up to peer out the door. In the dim moonlight, she'd seen something about a foot high staring at her. It took her a minute to realize the creature was a possum. It ran away when it saw her. She hadn't known they lived this far north. And it was a big one.

Evangeline had no idea what time it was, but people were up. She could hear noises from them outside her door. She'd been given one of the small houses. All to herself. What a luxury, where other people were sharing.

Stretching, she tried to get some of the kinks out of her body. Her shoulders still ached from carrying the heavy pack. She had no salve to put on them. Her few belongings burned in the fire.

She'd left the window partly open, grateful for the fresh air. She'd always slept with a window open, until she moved up here to Roosevelt's warehouse. Where her room had no windows to leave open.

She could smell that the cooks had a fire going already. It looked dim and gray outside. How could people stand this part of the world? Always so cold and gray.

Evangeline shivered in the coolness of the morning. She dug around in her pack and found a light jacket. She grabbed the clothes she'd gotten from the pile yesterday before leaving the Zoo. Jeans that were too baggy for her, and a bit too long, but there hadn't been much choice. She could roll them up at least. And a t-shirt that would be the right weight if the day warmed up. It was still summer. Maybe.

She quickly changed and put on the jacket. She hung yesterday's clothes on the two old wooden chairs. Maybe they'd air out some. She should wash them today, once she found out how to do that. Maybe someone had some soap and a large tub.

Evangeline left her door open, hoping the small house would warm up some. She went and stood by the cook's fire, rubbing her hands.

"Here dearie," said one of the older women. She pushed a broken handled mug of steaming coffee into Evangeline's hands.

"Thank you."

"Enjoy it. This is the last of our coffee. The rest got burned up with the food storage warehouse."

"I will savor it then," said Evangeline.

The woman nodded and shuffled back to her table. She returned to cutting up apples which then got added to a pot of what looked like oatmeal. It smelled like the porridge Evangeline had had as a child. Warm and cinnamony. It smelled like home.

Evangeline stood in front of the blazing fire. A tear threatened to run down her cheek. She wiped it away and sipped at the hot coffee, trying to calm herself.

She hadn't thought of her childhood home for a very long time. Before they'd had to leave the island. The sea had swallowed up her home and then came Hurricane Tallulah, which wiped out everything.

Her family had fled to what was left of Florida. That horrible, inhospitable armpit of a place. Biting insects, spiders and snakes everywhere you turned. People were mean and there was no work. That was where Evangeline had learned to fight.

As her people moved across the south, Evangeline had picked up bits of magic everywhere she went. They went up the panhandle into Georgia, then across Alabama and Mississippi. They followed the shoreline of the ever-hungry sea into Louisiana and finally found a home again in Texas. Their journey began when she was seven and ended eleven years later in a dry dusty small town.

She learned from priests and priestesses, curanderos and shamans. She discovered that deities and mythological creatures had re-entered the world. She spent a decade learning from Mawu/Lisa. And learning how to defend herself and others.

She never wanted to be a priestess. She'd chosen to be a magical bodyguard. To use her powers to defend those who could pay her. Those whose wealth could provide a home for her. She spent many years happily employed in Texas.

Until Roosevelt lured her away with his large amount of cash. And a promise she'd never have to worry about losing her home again. Look where that had led her.

Evangeline sipped the hot coffee, tasting every bean that

had gone into making it. She would indeed savor every last drop.

She needed to leave. To find her way somewhere else that was safe. And not in the middle of a damn wilderness.

She'd done her best at her work. Although failing to keep Roosevelt alive, but she was not stupid enough to believe she could defeat bombs dropped from planes. Having helped get these people to safety, there was now no reason left for her to stay. She'd simply decline Morrigu's offer and move on. To where, she didn't know.

Maybe south. To what was left of California. She'd heard it was hard to get in. They limited immigrants. It would be warmer at least. And there was money there. California was wealthy. She could go back to being a sorcerer and a bodyguard.

She'd need to find better clothes though. No one would believe she was good at what she did looking like this. Maybe she could find work on the way down the coast. At least buy something nicer.

Because living in the wilderness wasn't going to work for her. Even with a goddess.

Evangeline looked around. Morrigu was nowhere in sight. She'd left the fire last night and wandered off into the woods. As if looking for something.

Several people were still crowded around a table. Using tools on something electrical. At least that's what it looked like. With their focus, Evangeline didn't doubt they'd have power going within a week. They looked as if they had been at it all night.

Two of the cooks were talking about the need for more meat. They were making a list of animals that someone had to find and begin raising. And the crops that would need to be grown.

Evangeline was impressed. These people were willing to begin at the start of civilization. To learn how to grow food. To generate their own power. Probably to weave their own fabric too. To recreate their lives anew.

She was too, but not from ancient history. She appreciated running water and instant heat and electronics. Not having a wristband bothered her more than she could say. Not having a purpose. The magic she'd learned was mostly defensive. She was of no use here. Morrigu didn't need her, not really.

And even if they did manage to find the resources for Morrigu's war, Evangeline was of no use there. She wasn't a warrior. Her magic wasn't for going on the offensive. Not at the scale of planes and bombs. Her skills were useless. She completely understood Damon's hesitation. He felt useless in that situation also.

She hadn't seen him since early last night. All day he'd been strangely withdrawn. He needed to leave too. Why didn't he?

There was so much she didn't understand about these northerners. They were such a closed, reserved people. Evangeline couldn't read them. Roosevelt had been different. Open and outgoing. His emotions on his sleeve. She would miss him. He had been decent and kind.

She slowly became aware that more people were awake and coming to the fire. It was getting crowded. Evangeline moved away and began to walk one of the well-worn paths, sipping from the mug of coffee as she went.

There were tall trees all around. Evergreens. She didn't know what kind they were. Everything around here was alien to her. She'd learned a few of the herbs, but that was about it.

Off of the path the bases of the trees were cluttered with bushes and dried weeds. Or maybe they weren't weeds. She didn't recognize any of them. She passed through a clearing where there was a small mountain of thorny vines. Dark purple berries grew there, although she didn't know if they were edible.

Some of the deciduous trees and bushes were beginning to turn, their leaves yellowing. Occasionally, she saw a tree that was brilliant red or orange. When did winter begin up here? She'd arrived at the beginning of spring. The days had grown longer and almost warm.

Now, the nights were cool and days only less so. Someone had told her that fall, winter and spring just meant nine months of rain. She shuddered at the thought.

She needed to leave. Tomorrow. She'd put everything in the pack tonight. Grab some extra food. Tell Morrigu she wasn't needed. Then leave before dawn.

Evangeline continued following the path. She sipped the coffee, reveling in the intense bitter flavor. Who knew when she'd find some again? Most places weren't as well stocked as Morrigu and Roosevelt's kitchens had been.

The path led down to the water. To the edge of the sea that she could never seem to get away from. The air smelled of salt and fish. At least Morrigu's people could find food here.

There. Through the mist, lay a couple of islands. Another shore was visible across the bay. Boats sat out on the water, not moving. People must be fishing.

Evangeline was startled by a movement on the nearby shore. A woman walked there. No, a deity. Almost shimmering in the grayness of morning.

As the deity came closer, Evangeline saw that the spirit had black skin and long coily-curly black hair, hanging loose about her hips. Throughout her hair was braided strands of pearls. She wore a loose blue fabric wrapped around her ample hips, leaving her breasts bare. Through the reeds, she walked, her feet bare.

Evangeline just stood and stared.

"You have brought me an offering. Thank you," said the spirit, taking Evangeline's cup and tasting the coffee. Then she handed it back to Evangeline.

"Who are you?" asked Evangeline.

"Do you not recognize me? I am your mother. The mother of all the oceans, the great mother."

"Yemaya?" asked Evangeline.

"Yes, my child."

"But why are you here? This far north."

"Why are you?"

"It was a mistake," said Evangeline.

"I don't believe in mistakes. It is part of your path."

"How can that be? I don't belong here."

"Always you have sought a home, never had you been willing to take a risk and stay."

"My whole life has been a risk. My work has always kept me moving. And Texas wasn't a home. It was dried out and scorched. I wasn't happy there."

"You will not find happiness by looking in a place, but by looking at the people who surround you. You refuse to risk trusting people," said Yemaya. "Drink."

"Why?"

"It will help."

"Did you put something in my coffee?"

"Nothing that you don't need."

Evangeline sniffed the coffee. There was only one sip left,

she drained the cup. It tasted a bit saltier than before. A surge of energy poured through her.

"You must find home by bonding with other people. By trusting again. Your family is all gone. Taken by floods or disease or old age. You must create a new family. Stay here. I claim you as one of mine."

"I hate this place," said Evangeline.

"Learn to love it. It is extraordinarily beautiful. See the way the fog hugs the water. The tide caresses the grasses growing at its edge. Hear the call of the eagle, just before she dives for a salmon. Stay and learn the ways of this land. You have always been shut inside, never understanding the life of the wild and the earth. Not feeling its rhythms. It is time to learn. To change. To grow."

Evangeline stood and stared into Yemaya's eyes. They were a stormy gray-blue. And the irises and pupils had a spiral of light that swirled through them. The longer she stared, the more she began to believe it was right to stay and help these people.

She was thinking that as she slid to the marshy grass and blacked out.

16

CADY

Cady woke with the sunlight streaming in her window. She'd been having deep dreams again. Something that hadn't happened since she was a child. Prophetic dreams. It must be all the change of moving.

She'd seen that woman from the Zoo. The sorcerer who'd caught them in her magical net. But the woman had been old. Surrounded by others to whom she was telling ancient stories. Firelight had flickered on the sorcerer's face, but Cady hadn't been able to hear what was being said.

Cady jumped when Monster thundered in through the cat door, leapt down from his shelf on the wall and jumped up on her bed in two bounds. Yowling and demanding attention.

"Well, good morning to you too."

She petted him. He felt damp from the dew.

Finally, she got out of bed and went outside to relieve herself. No matter how little liquid she drank at night, her body could just barely make it till morning anymore. This must be what getting old was about.

She walked back inside, pouring water to wash her hands

and face. Then stretched out some of her stiffness. She changed into brown pants that tied in front and a soft shirt that had been dyed green. The clothes had been a gift from Joaquin's family. They spun the wool from their sheep and alpaca and wove it into the finest fabric. Then made clothes for nearly everyone in the village, in exchange for others' services.

She poured clean water into a saucepan and switched on a burner that Mateo had found for her. All the finished houses had been wired to a solar and wind system that Logan had created. His father had made the one back in the old village and Logan had maintained it. Logan had made this system with a few modifications so it would work better. Cady now had lights and electricity.

Not enough to heat her house this winter, he'd told her, for that there was wood. He would begin expanding the system once everyone was hooked in. Next winter everyone would have enough power to heat with his system.

Cady was grateful for everything this house had. She'd underestimated the power of friendship.

Digging around in her packets of dried herbs, Cady found some mint, rose petals and bee balm, pouring a small bit of each into one of her cloth tea bags. There wasn't much of the mint left, but the roots she'd brought from the old village were beginning to grow strongly. She put the bag into her clear blue mug.

Out on the lake, a patch of fog drifted by. Cady could see at least three spirits swirling around in it. They looked like air spirits, white and wispy with wings and long flowing white hair.

She'd seen one up close once. The spirit had looked at her with its ice blue eyes. Cady had been chilled to the bone. Then it shrieked like a haunted wind and was gone.

The area surrounding the lake, and the lake itself, was overflowing with deities, mythological creatures and spirits of all kinds. Some of the villagers were having a difficult time with that. Nearly everyone was discovering long denied magical powers within themselves.

Cady had found she had a knack for starting fires. Just breathing on a stack of wood seemed to do it nowadays. That might have been from hanging around a dragon.

She spent her afternoons chatting with Onyx. He had a wealth of information about ancient times and told her wonderful stories. Of course, he'd missed the rise and fall of entire empires, so he wasn't any good with recent history. The thing that surprised her was that it didn't sound like humans had changed much in a couple thousand years or more.

She poured the hot water over the tea and went outside while it steeped. Monster followed her. He did that all the time now, still unsure about this new place or perhaps he just enjoyed her company as much as she did his.

There were still some huckleberries on the bushes, so she ate several. The village would be short of fruit for a few years, unless they found more still growing around here.

Several people had brought berry canes and strawberry roots. Others had brought small fruit trees, planting them in the center of the village, for everyone to share. It would take years before they began to bear fruit.

She might not even be alive that many years in the future. Then again, none of them might. Life was uncertain.

She returned to the house, removed the tea bag and began to sip her tea. There was a knock at the door.

"Come in."

"Good morning," said Beth.

"Well, hello. Would you like a cup of tea?"

"No, I've had plenty already this morning. I've been up since the middle of the night."

"Couldn't sleep?" asked Cady, sitting down at the table with her tea.

Beth sat down in the other chair. Her hair was perfect. Straight and down to her shoulders, light brown in color. Her blue shirt and pants were clean and unwrinkled. The same cut as Cady's except Beth's looked better on her. Brown leather shoes, clean and without scuffs. Somehow, she looked tidy and well put together, while Cady always looked like an unmade bed. Which was what her house looked like too. She'd bet that Beth's house was well organized as Beth was.

"I slept for a while, but woke after another dream."

"Bad dream?"

"No, just intense and puzzling. Like all my dreams lately."

"You're not alone. There's so much magic swirling around in the air some days it makes me dizzy."

"Is that what it is?" asked Beth. "I've never really believed in magic, you know."

"I know. but haven't you noticed? Inexplicable things are happening. Even to people who don't believe in magic. Look how quickly all the houses got built. The crops are growing much faster, stronger and healthier than in the old village. Nearly everyone is getting along. I've not heard one disagreement since we arrived."

"I thought that was just because we all felt like a village. We all pulled together for the move, helping each other and people are going out of their way more to be kind to each other."

"It's more than that. The water's cleaner, the air is fresher. The food tastes better. People who are weaving, knitting or sewing clothes—it's like they have magical fingers.

Even the animals are growing healthier and larger. So are the kids. I can start a fire in my little wood stove just by blowing on it."

"Then why am I having such intense dreams?"

"Because you're repressing magic," said Cady.

It was true of herself, too. Her dreams had become more intense of late. What sort of magic was she holding back on?

"But I don't have any magic," said Beth.

"I believe everyone has magic. You simply haven't found an outlet for it yet," said Cady.

Beth looked shocked. As if someone had slapped her.

"So, even if I don't believe in magic, I've got it anyway? That makes no sense."

"Magic doesn't care. It uses all of us."

"You speak about it as if it's a living thing," said Beth.

"Look at that fog, drifting across the lake. You can barely see it, if you were in the middle of it, it wouldn't be very visible, not like a rock. Or touchable. You can't taste it. Yet it exists all the same. It moves, it takes shape, thickens, thins. It's not alive either, but it affects us. If you were in a boat out there, trying to find your way to shore, the fog would have an effect on you. Whether it's alive or not, it exists and denying that it exists means nothing to the fog. It doesn't diminish it."

"So you don't believe the magic is alive?"

"I know it moves through us. That wherever it's strongest, there are deities and spirits. Or maybe it's the other way around. I don't know if it's alive. Before now, I've never had a great deal of magic. Just the power to find things. It feels like the magic, if it is alive, likes us and wants the village to thrive here."

Beth sat back in her chair and was silent. Thinking.

Cady sipped her tea. She'd forgotten to put honey in it,

and took a spoonful from the jar on the table, stirring it in. Waiting for Beth to sort things out in her mind.

Monster came in the door and rubbed against her chair. Cady picked him up and put him on her lap. He purred and purred.

"How do I stop repressing my magic then?"

"You start by believing magic exists. Look for it. Notice how the people around you have changed. See how the village has changed. Look at what's different in this area than the old village. We are surrounded by deities and spirits. I saw three unicorns in the woods the other day. There are faeries who live on the other side of the ravine, they're difficult to spot, blending in with the trees and they're very reclusive, but they're there. Water sprites live in the lake. Magic is everywhere here. Find it. Once you can do that, your own magical gifts will be more apparent."

"But what sort of magic am I likely to have?" asked Beth.

"I have no idea. I'm still finding out what I have."

"Will I be able to hide it?"

"Why would you want too?" asked Cady.

"Liam won't like it. And the kids. ..."

"All of them are probably coming into their own magic too. If you can't lead them in this, there's no hope that they'll accept what's happening."

"I'm not the leader in our family."

"Well, everything's changing here by this lake. Maybe that should. You're a leader in this community."

"I have something to offer. I'm skilled at organizing."

"Well, you must have something to offer your family. Acceptance of their magic is huge. And, I'm not one to talk here because I never married, but the best marriages I've seen are partnerships. Where the leadership is shared. We all change throughout our lives. Maybe it's time your marriage changed. You should talk to Liam. Otherwise this is going to be a hard road for all of you. And we've all seen enough hard roads."

"He won't listen. He's stubborn."

"Well, talk to your kids. They need to understand what's happening to them."

"I can do that," said Beth.

There was another knock at her door. Two people before breakfast. That *was* unusual.

"Come in," said Cady.

Mazzy came in the door.

"Good morning," she said to both of them.

"Good morning," said Cady, "what can I do for you?"

"I'm having a problem. Although, I don't know if Beth wants to hear about it. It concerns magic and I know she's not a believer."

Beth made a move to get up.

"No," said Cady, "you need to stay and hear this. It's the only way you'll learn."

"Okay," said Beth, "if you think it will help."

"Yes," said Cady. "Would you like some tea?"

"I'd love some," said Mazzy.

Cady motioned for Mazzy to take her chair and put on more water to heat. She pulled another mug out. Then put more herbs in a second teabag. She poured the hot water into the green cup that had a picture of a hummingbird on it and her own cup. She needed another cup of tea.

She set a wooden bowl of red-green apples on the table. Sharine had found a wild apple tree growing next to an abandoned ruin of a house. It had been loaded with apples and she'd made five trips to gather them all and then distribute them around the village.

Beth took one and said, "Thanks."

Mazzy said, "I don't think I can eat another apple. I've had so many over the last few days. I can't wait until we can harvest some of our vegetables."

Cady set a cup of tea in front of Mazzy, and added honey to her own. Grabbing an apple, she walked over to the small table by her bed and set the tea on it. Then sat on the bed, facing the two of them, crossing her legs and resting her elbows on her knees.

"So, what is your problem, Mazzy?"

She took a bite of the apple. The juice filled her mouth. It was tart and sweet at the same time. Her empty belly rumbled appreciatively.

Mazzy hesitated for a minute, running her fingers through her short, black hair. She normally looked in complete control, but her clothes were wrinkled and her hair unbrushed.

"In the old village, I occasionally saw a deity. Not often. But here, I see one every time I turn around. A different one. And I'm seeing other things. Dragons, of all kinds, and not just Onyx. All of us can see and touch him, he's real. I've seen Enenra, smoke monsters. And Kitsune, they're intelligent, sometimes trickster foxes. And so many more spirits."

"What's wrong with that?" asked Cady.

"Something is wrong with me."

"Nothing is wrong with you. This place is filled with magic. More magic than the old village. For some reason, deities and spirits have gathered here. I don't know why, but you're not seeing things."

"There's something else," said Mazzy, shifting awkwardly in the chair. She looked very uncomfortable.

"Okay," said Cady.

"When I talk to people, they always agree with me now. No one ever argues. It's as if my words are suddenly magic and can convince anyone. I got Joe to admit that the sky was green yesterday. And he always argues with me about everything."

"That's a powerful gift to have."

"What if I'm wrong? No one will argue me out of anything."

"I just did," said Cady, taking another large bite of the apple.

"So, I'm not imagining that my words are suddenly golden?"

"Probably not. We're all coming into powers we've never had before."

"But my words won't work on everyone?"

"Well, I saw your thinking was flawed. I can't speak for anyone else."

"Being able to convince people nearly all the time is a heavy responsibility," said Mazzy, sipping her tea.

"One I think you're up to carrying. It means you'll think before you speak, knowing your words have a great weight to them."

Cady set the apple core on her table and stirred the tea, mixing any unmelted honey in. She sipped it.

"You said 'we're all coming into powers we've never had before'. Who is we?"

"Much of the village. I don't know about everyone, but there's a lot of magic going on. Chickens are laying more eggs. Goats giving more milk and it's richer. Crops are growing more rapidly and are healthier than in the old village. Cloth being woven is softer, and the weavers are weaving more quickly. Houses are still being built with an unthinkable speed. And they're being hooked up to the power faster than planned. Sharine says everyone and their animals are healthier here. There's been fewer people needing to see her and she actually has spare time. Besides all those things, I can now start a fire by blowing on the kindling in my wood stove. I know other people are experiencing magic, they're just not talking about it. There are still people in the village who don't believe in magic," said Cady.

Mazzy looked at Beth.

Beth spoke. "It's true, I used to not believe in magic. I started to when Cady found Sam. And then who can deny that Onyx exists. I've been having strange dreams. And my kids, they're doing things that are impossible. Seeing into each other's minds. Making toys vanish and reappear. The other day, one of them made a bowl of strawberries show up on the table. Completely out of season. We all ate them, they tasted wonderful. I don't know what to make of all this."

"Did Liam have a strawberry?" asked Cady.

"Yes, although he didn't see them suddenly appear. He thought I'd found them somewhere near the village. I tried to explain and he looked at me like I had two heads. I quit trying then."

Cady nodded.

Mazzy said, "So, how are these deities different than Morrigu? I don't see any of them trying to change people's lives like she did in the Zoo."

"Morrigu has more power for one thing. I'm not sure why, maybe it's because she's a war goddess and humanity's endless wars have fed her well. She's taken a more physical form than many of these deities and spirits, sort of like Onyx. She clearly wanted to be involved with people. The other deities remain separate from us. They may or may not even see us. Or we might be beneath their notice—lesser beings."

"Is that likely to change?" asked Beth.

"I have no idea. Magic has been in the world since I was a young girl. The village I lived in then didn't acknowledge it. When I ran away to the Zoo, most of those people didn't believe in magic. They just said I had a knack for finding things. It wasn't until Morrigu came along that things began to change there. By then, I was ready to leave. I think this explosion of magic is limited to this lake, but I could be wrong. It's more concentrated here, certainly."

"Onyx said he found one area, on the other side of the lake, where humans have lived recently, but it was abandoned," said Mazzy.

"Was he looking for other people?" asked Cady.

"He goes flying every morning. I asked him where and why and he said he wants to keep us safe. So he flies over the surrounding area to see if there are any threats."

Cady sipped her tea. She hadn't known that.

Mazzy said, "I think we should talk about the magic at our next village meeting. Everyone should know what's going on."

"I agree," said Beth. "Liam isn't going to believe me. He needs to hear it from everyone else."

"The two of you know there will be consequences to such a discussion."

"Like what?" asked Mazzy.

"The people who don't believe in magic will be afraid. In the past, fearful people have killed those they didn't understand. Depending on how many of those in the village refuse to believe, they could cause large problems."

"You mean, if they're in the majority, they could decide to

kill us? Well, we won't know until we talk about it," said Mazzy. "I think they're the minority."

"I'm not saying we shouldn't talk about it, just to be aware there are consequences. And to prepare for them," said Cady.

Mazzy said, "Okay, I'll talk to Sharine and Joaquin. See if we can figure out how to handle anyone who causes trouble. Maybe add something to the village charter, in the harassment section."

"I think we should encourage them to leave the village," said Beth.

Cady looked at Beth. She felt shocked Beth would suggest such a thing.

"Well, I do," said Beth.

"What if Liam decides to leave?" asked Mazzy.

"Good riddance. He's being a jerk. He doesn't believe me, or even listen to me anymore. Spends nearly all his time in the workshop, making shoes for people who don't need new ones. Or else he's off somewhere and I can't find him. I'm taking care of four kids, and the house, and foraging for food, and cooking it. I'm not sure what I need him for. When he does come home, he just makes fun of what I say or he ignores me."

Cady looked up to see a deity peering in the window. She had wild black hair, blue skin and four arms. A necklace of human skulls hung around her neck. When Cady met the deity's black eyes, the goddess stuck out her tongue. There was no mistaking her, Kali had come to their village.

What did her presence mean?

Cady tried not to panic.

DAMON

DAMON STOOD IN THE CENTER OF THE VILLAGE. SIX MEN were building a central meeting hall over the fire pit. They had cut and peeled the logs and were hoisting them up on the circular frame they had built. The sides would be mostly open to vent the smoke, but the top needed to be covered to keep the winter rains off.

Only one of the men knew what he was doing, so there was a lot of arguing going on. The others seemed to think Karan was just being a perfectionist.

Damon walked over and said, "As of now, I appoint Karan to be head of this project. He understands engineering and I really don't want this building to fall down on Morrigu's head. Or to leak rain on the cooks. Understand?"

The men nodded and went back to work.

He walked back to the table he'd been working at. Someone had found him an ancient pad of paper and a pencil. He missed his wristband.

Using paper to organize all these people was cumbersome. There were groups of people scavenging for wire and other things that Carlos and Martina needed to create their electric system. Nearby ruined houses and power lines provided some of it. For some things, the groups had to go farther out to what had once been main streets with businesses to search.

Other small groups were trying to barter for animals from the farms they'd passed. And getting information about raising those animals. Still others were off hunting for food to cook for the next few days.

Morrigu had sent two scouts back to the Zoo. To see what damage Collins had done. They had returned to report that the Zoo had been leveled. No buildings left standing and plenty of holes in the ground. A total loss.

Damon watched her reaction. Morrigu said nothing. There was no fury even. Apparently, she had expected the news that the Zoo was gone.

The Goddess sat there on a sawed off tree stump, almost looked as if she was carved out of stone. Damon could seen her thinking. Taking everything into consideration. Then she'd risen and walked off into the woods alone.

Everyone had stood around, looking at him. Waiting for him to give them some direction.

"You two go and get some food and sleep, he said to the scouts. The rest of you must have been assigned work. If you don't have work, those who are growing food for us need help. There are also openings for people willing to build looms and weave fabric. We're going to need warmer coats soon. But first, the looms need building. Hopefully by then, we'll have some sheep, and wool to weave with. There's no shortage of work to do around here."

Everyone left quickly after that. Damon rubbed his face. So few of them knew what they were doing and neither did he.

There was too much to learn to support the whole

community. Building, growing food, raising livestock, creating electricity from the air and sun. And more. They had no one who knew much about healing. And how were they supposed to grow food? Winter was coming. The sun would disappear, replaced with nine months of rain. And Morrigu wanted a war when they didn't even know how to feed themselves.

Damon felt unfocused and overwhelmed with all the things that needed to happen immediately. He paced around the center of the village trying to think of what he might be missing. What crucial thing had he overlooked? And how were they going to buy weapons? The local economy probably existed on barter, but what was left of the wide world had reverted back to gold. That was the currency these days. Maybe jewels or art. But all of Morrigu's assets had been destroyed with the Zoo.

Morrigu walked into the center of the village and stood next to him.

She said, "We need to find someone nearby with weapons and steal them."

Damon looked at her, not allowing his mouth to drop open with shock.

She continued, "We can gather all the nearby weapons and begin training our people. Collect any new people who want to join us in our battle on the Eastside."

"We can't even feed ourselves," said Damon. "How are we going to track down weapons?"

"Before our systems went out, Roosevelt had people he was buying arms from."

"Local people?"

"Not all of them. But Jack, one of his advisors, had a hacker make a list of the arms dealer's other clients. Some of them were local. Jack said he still has the list. It was on paper."

Damon said, "So, we break into their storage areas, risking our lives and killing a few of them, stealing weapons, ammo and disappearing. Then what?"

"We keep doing it. For as long as it takes. All winter if need be. We train people hard. Create an army," said Morrigu.

"Even with an army, how do we attack Collins? He's got aircraft and bombs, any one of which could obliterate our entire army in seconds."

"We don't attack him. We meet with those whose land borders Collin's little fiefdom. There was Morietti, and another one. We offer to combine our army with theirs and overthrow Collins."

"Will that be enough? What if they don't want to fight Collins? What if they're fine with things the way they are?" asked Damon

"We don't need to fight. All I need is the threat. We will demand a meeting with Collins or we will attack and obliterate him. All I need is to get into the same room with Collins and he's dead."

"What if Collins won't meet with anyone?" Damon asked. "I wouldn't. Not with his power and security."

"Then we fight." She stared at him, her green eyes blazing.

There was no talking her out of this. Morrigu would have her revenge.

"I'll talk to Jack, find a couple of men to scout things out before we plan a mission. And get Gregor back to training people. When they're not trying to build a place for us to eat, and trying to keep us all fed and clothed."

Morrigu said, "You are right, our people are not farmers and shepherds. I think we should steal what we need. Clothes, food and weapons."

"I'm not sure we have enough people to do that. Without losing a lot of them fighting."

"Don't get caught," said Morrigu.

"Things don't always turn out that way. I was there in the Zoo back when that's what the gangs did. Before you came there. Stealing to survive. Of all of the people I ran with, only two people are still alive."

"Who?" asked Morrigu, cocking her head.

"One of the villagers who Evangeline caught, back in the Zoo. The older woman, Cady, who was shot in the leg. She got out early, when she was still young. And myself. Everyone else from that time died or got out of the Zoo early on, like Cady. Stealing for survival is a hard road these days, too many losses. You won't build your army up that way."

"All right, we'll strike a balance. Steal weapons and grow everything else."

"That would be better. Because at least half of these people were support staff in the Zoo. Cooks, cleaners and all that. They aren't warriors and there's no way Gregor can make them into warriors. At best, he'd be able to teach them how to defend themselves if we're attacked. At best."

"Well, go back to training anyone who has a possibility of becoming a warrior. Let the others focus on sustaining the rest of us. They will need to be trained to defend themselves. None of this comes without a risk of us being attacked again," said Morrigu.

"I can do that after we've got hold of seeds to plant and animals to raise for food and wool. And structures built for us. Otherwise, we won't last through the winter."

Morrigu said, "Do what needs to be done, but send scouts out to find likely places to steal weapons from."

Damon nodded. As if that would be easy. Anyone with a

large amount of weapons would have them under strong security. Still, he'd talk to Jack when he got back. At the moment, Jack was with those seeking seeds and animals. He'd agreed to negotiate, having few other skills to offer.

There weren't enough warriors to send out right now, anyway. Not until everyone returned. They were either out hunting for food, trying to barter for animals or guarding folks collecting wire and equipment. Damon would not leave everyone here undefended.

Morrigu began to leave and then turned back.

"Do you know what this village is called?" she asked.

"No."

"It's called Paradise Grove. There's a sign down by the water with an arrow pointing this way. I love this place. It reminds me of my home. Before humans cut down too many trees. But if this was paradise, why did the villagers leave?"

Damon said, "They had a seer. They probably saw us coming."

"Perhaps," she said. "It's of no matter. They weren't warriors. We need warriors and I will find them."

Morrigu turned and walked back into the forest, soon vanishing behind the bushes and trees. Damon went back to his papers. There were twenty-five fighters gone right now. Leaving only twenty with the village. That made him nervous, but everything everyone was doing was important. And there were timelines on it all. They needed food now. They needed food in the future. They would need warmth in the winter. And they needed to be safe.

He heard a yell.

"Incoming! Take cover!"

Followed by noise in the bushes.

"Get down!" yelled Damon to everyone around him. He

pulled his rifle off the table, thankful he'd kept it nearby. "Grab a weapon if you've got one."

People scuttled behind trees and behind buildings. He heard weapons firing and more rustling. Then Gregor and Eamon ran through the clearing and took cover behind a house. Damon joined them.

"How many?"

"Ten, maybe fifteen."

"Who?"

"Local yokels. Not pros. But good shots. They got Cal," Gregor said.

Seven more people came through the clearing. One of them, a big man, dumped a deer carcass on the ground near the fire, and kept running to find cover.

Damon raised his rifle to fire, but Gregor said, "They're ours. Not going to leave dinner behind. The others are wearing camo. Probably surrounding us. I'll watch your back."

"Eyes out!" yelled Gregor.

Damon could see the other fighters, the ones who'd already been in or near the village, circling around. Two of them got off shots. Then he heard an unearthly scream.

Morrigu walked into the clearing dragging a man by his short hair and two of her guards marched another in front of her.

"Who are you?" she demanded.

Neither man answered.

"Why are you here, why did you attack us?"

Silence.

Some of Morrigu's people came out of hiding. Damon and the other guards stayed put, watching for a continuation of the attack.

Morrigu pulled the man upright. He shrieked again. Then she began to peel the skin off his face with a knife, in strips.

Damon shut out the screams, looking away.

At one point, she stopped, and yelled, "You will watch this. You will watch your friend die. This is what becomes of those who dare to attack Morrigu's people. I am a goddess. You cannot kill me. I destroy anyone who dares to attempt to hurt me or mine. You are an insect I crush beneath my boot."

The first man continued screaming until he lost consciousness. He probably wasn't dead yet. Damon hoped she'd kill him soon and be done with it.

"Damon," she said.

He came out from behind the house and walked to her.

"Do we have a place to confine this one until he wakes?"

"We don't have anyplace yet, no," he said.

"Pity. I'll just have to kill him and be done with it. There's more pain he could endure."

She sliced the man's throat and took a yellow mug off the table, tossing out whatever liquid was in it. Then she held the cup at the man's neck, filling it with blood, which she drank, letting it run down her face.

The other man had already paled and was hyperventilating from fear. Watching Morrigu drink his friend's blood made him vomit.

Morrigu finished drinking and slapped the mug down on the table with a thunk.

"Throw his body on the fire. We will have human for dinner tonight."

Two guards did as she asked. Then she turned to the other prisoner, who looked ready to pass out.

"I will let you go. You will spread the word wide and far about what happens to those who enter my territory with evil intent. I take care of mine. I am a warrior goddess and all who oppose me will die terrible deaths. Do not return."

She motioned to the guards to let him go. The man took about one second to find his balance. Then fled back the way he'd come.

"That was quite a performance," said Damon.

"Yes, it was good, wasn't it? But it will be effective. Those who hear his tale, won't bother us."

"What about those who don't believe it?"

"They will come to us, challenging us. We will welcome them as warriors."

The guards brought Cal's body to the fire, stripping it of weapons, ammunition and boots. Then his body, too was consigned to the fire.

Damon left the area. He felt weary of the scent of burning bodies. When Morrigu and Roosevelt had finally made their peace, he'd thought that burning bodies would be done. And it had, for a very long time, unless someone died of an accident or illness. Now, it had begun again. It would get worse before it got better. Hadn't enough people died?

He sat on an old rotting log and put his head in his hands. Tired of taking other lives. Exhausted from fighting and running. He just wanted it to end.

But they were going to war and it sickened him.

18

EVANGELINE

EVANGELINE WOKE TO FIND HERSELF LYING ON THE SOFT, damp grass. Where was she? Who was she? She sat up to see water, salty water by the smell. She was on a shore. Tall evergreen trees towered above her. She didn't know what kind of trees they were.

Standing, she startled a heron. The bird's ungainly body took off with a thump, thump of wings, as the long neck folded into a compressed S-shape, and the heron tucked in its long legs. She felt just as ungainly, trying to find her balance.

Whatever hit her must have been some powerful magic. Then she remembered Yemaya with those stormy gray eyes. And the work the goddess had given her to do.

Evangeline rubbed her face then pulled her hair back. She found a strip of cloth in her pants pocket and tied those long braids back into a bundle. She was never going to be able to take care of her hair properly here. Perhaps it was time to let it go.

There were a lot of things she'd never be able to do here, like have her beautiful clothes again. Or be connected into a network, always able to call for backup. Or see the people that were left in her family. That life was gone.

Evangeline found the empty mug that the cook, whose name she didn't even know, had given her. With the last cup of coffee Evangeline might ever have.

Picking it up, she walked back to the village, passing the sign that read *Paradise Grove*. Well, she would turn it into her paradise. Whatever that took.

As she moved down the path beneath the evergreens, the dimness of the forest surrounded her. The village needed to make or find boats. They could fish for food. She'd seen other boats out on the water fishing.

And she needed to learn about the local plants. The former villagers had been thriving. They must have been able to get everything they needed. Morrigu and Roosevelt's people would just have to learn how to do that. There must be books somewhere in the village that identified plants. She would search them out. See what the plants could do for food, for healing.

Evangeline startled a little brown rabbit, which hopped a short distance and disappeared into the bushes. Small birds of some kind twittered all around her as they moved from shrub to small tree. She knew the short trees. They were maples of some sort, their leaves turning orange and crimson with the cooler weather. They struggled to find light beneath the taller trees.

In a meadow grew mounds of brambles, bearing what she'd learned were blackberries. Very tasty. She ate several. Her stomach was grumbling. When had she last eaten?

Evangeline didn't know how long she'd been out. She couldn't even see the sun in this part of the woods, so couldn't see how low it was in the sky.

When she made it back to the village, it seemed like an alien place. Everyone was busy. No one greeted her. She could have been a ghost.

It looked like they'd gotten all the timbers up on the roof of the meeting area. Two men were on top filling the cracks between the logs with mud or something.

The three main cooks were working, helped by two other people. It seemed like the cooks never stopped. There were a lot of mouths to feed.

Evangeline went to the tub of warm, soapy water and washed her mug, rinsed it and set it on the table to air dry.

She went to the older woman who'd given her coffee. The cook was stoutly built, but muscular beneath the extra weight. Evangeline had watched her heft huge pots filled with food. The woman had long red hair piled on top of her head and secured with two sharp ornamental sticks.

"Thank you for the coffee, it was wonderful."

The woman scrunched up her face, as if puzzled.

Then said, "That was yesterday, but you're welcome."

"It was yesterday? I fell asleep down by the lake. I must have been really tired."

"You must have. You slept through gunshots and everything."

"Gunshots?" asked Evangeline.

The cook filled her in.

"I was exhausted. Too many days without sleep. I'm sorry, I don't even know your name."

"Angie."

"Angie, I'm Evangeline."

"I know," said the cook. "There's some leftover roasted deer from last night, better grab some before it goes into this afternoon's soup."

"Thank you."

Evangeline took a hunk of the meat, grateful for the food. It was chewy and tasted like most roasted meat. A bit dry though. At least they'd gotten a refrigeration system working for the cooks. The tech people had only found enough wire to run electricity in a small area so far. Evangeline found a jug of water and poured some into the clean yellow mug. After drinking the cool mineral-flavored water, she washed and rinsed the mug again.

Damon was out at a central table surrounded by paperwork, where he'd been ever since they'd arrived in the village. He had his head down on the table and was snoring. He probably hadn't slept in days either.

She didn't want to disturb him, but then he woke suddenly, sat up and looked around as if shocked out of sleep by a bad dream.

Evangeline went over and sat down on the split log bench on the other side of the table. The bench was well worn from the previous villagers' bodies.

Damon was rubbing his face and he looked at her.

"Fell asleep," he mumbled.

"When was the last time you slept?" asked Evangeline.

"Last night. I slept long and deep. Couldn't take it anymore."

"You're probably still exhausted."

"Apparently," he said, frowning.

"When people were bringing books to you, were any of them about plants?"

"Plants. ..." he said.

"How to identify them. Local plants."

"There are a couple in my house. Cady's old house."

"Can I look at them?"

"Sure," he said. "Looking for anything in particular?"

"I need to be useful here. I can learn about what's growing nearby. What we can use for healing, what we can eat."

"You're a warrior, you're already useful."

"I'm done with that. I'm staying in this village. For good."

"How can you just turn around and say you're done with that?" Damon asked.

"I met a goddess yesterday, Yemaya. We had a ... discussion."

"And she trumps Morrigu?"

"I never agreed to work for Morrigu. She asked, but I never agreed. I will stay in this village. Be part of the community. Help it grow and thrive. But I'm done with fighting, war and being a bodyguard."

"I don't know how that'll work for you," said Damon. "We are going to war. Morrigu's made the first move."

"What did she do?" asked Evangeline.

Damon described the torture and why Morrigu had done it.

"She'll have every young punk for miles and miles around flocking to her. Anyone looking for violence and trouble. And we'll have to wrangle them into an army. While we're stealing arms from anyone who has them. This village is going to transform quickly."

"You really think so? Well, then it's a good thing I'm here to help keep the balance."

"Then, I'll put you in charge of training the non-warriors in self-defense. They're going to need it. They're used to dealing with disciplined guards not hormonal adolescents who are hot to prove themselves any way they can. And I can't spare Gregor for that. He'll have his hands full."

"Challenge accepted," she said. "I've always loved teaching people. This is going to be fun."

Damon put his head back down on the table.

"You're dreading this, aren't you?" asked Evangeline. She stood up, "Come on, take me to your house so I can get those books.

He rose and they began walking out of the center of the village.

"I'm not a soldier. I don't know how to fight a war on this scale," said Damon

He wasn't telling her everything. She could sense he was holding back some information. Well, it didn't concern her. She would do her work. Learn plants and teach people.

"I don't think anyone around here does. There hasn't been a war around here ever, has there?"

"Not in my lifetime," he said.

"So, there is no one suited for that job. Not in this part of the world. It's either you, or someone goes out into the wide world to find and hire some mercenary. I don't see that happening. No one around here has the gold to do that. Perhaps Morrigu could charm or threaten her way into a room on the other side of the planet, where she could find someone with that skillset. I think it's not likely. I doubt she can travel far."

Damon gazed off into the distance and said, "I know. It's me or if a miracle happens, her statement last night will bring someone. I'd be pleased to hand this over to someone else."

"Well, until that happens, you're it. So do what you're doing. Handle this job with integrity and grace."

He stared at her.

"I mean it. You're one of the most competent people I've ever met. You rise to confront every crisis. I've only been here a short time and there's been a lot of chaos. In the middle of it, there you are, straightening the tangles and making everything flow smoothly again."

"Doesn't feel that way to me. Feels like I'm jumping from the frying pan, to the fire, then into a damn volcano. And all my efforts just make things worse."

"You need more sleep."

They were at his house. They went inside and he showed her the bookcase of battered gardening books.

She found three that looked likely. One on native plants, another on garden plants and a third on weeds. The surrounding woods probably contained a mix of all three. Formerly a residential area, filled with houses, now ruined. People were still digging useful things out of the rubble in the woods here on a daily basis.

Nature had reclaimed this area with weeds and native plants and garden plants gone feral. She had some work ahead of her trying to figure out which plants were which.

"Now go back to bed and sleep," she said, standing in the doorway with the heavy books.

"I can't," he said.

"What is so critical that it can't wait a day?" she asked.

"I'm waiting for the people gathering wire to return. And the people finding animals to come back. And the hunters are due back. I need to be there."

"Everyone knows where to find you if there's an emergency. Everything else is just you sitting and waiting and letting panic defeat you. Sleep while you're waiting. Otherwise, you'll be useless to everyone."

Damon said, "You're right of course."

"I'm always right," said Evangeline.

She went out through the door, closing it behind her. Then

walked back to the center of the village and sat down at Damon's table.

Spreading out the books, she opened up the pages, taking care not to mix up the order of all the loose pages. The breeze kept trying to blow them away, so she finally got nearby rocks to hold down the pages as she read. She noticed Damon had done the same thing with all his papers.

After a while, she realized people had begun to populate the surrounding tables, eating lunch. She went over to the cooks and got a bowl of deer soup. There were a few root vegetables floating in it.

"What's this?" she asked Angie about a round one, brown with a white center.

"Oh, Jackie found a patch of burdock. Burdock root."

"Does Jackie know plants?"

Angie looked over to a tall, thin younger woman, about Evangeline's age.

Jackie nodded and said, "My mom used to scavenge for wild plants. I learned a little and I still remember some of it."

"Good. I've got some books on plants I'm trying to read. Can I come to you if I have questions?"

"Sure," said Jackie.

"Oh, and I'm in charge of teaching everyone how to defend themselves. We'll meet tonight, after you've cleaned up from cooking dinner. After you've eaten. Will that work?"

Angie raised her eyebrows.

"Is that necessary?"

"Yes," said Evangeline. "Being able to fend off an attack is important. Whether it's one of our enemies or some guy getting too friendly. I wish it wasn't so. You all need to learn and practice. Can you spread the word around?"

"I can do that," said Jackie.

"We'll be ready tonight," said Angie.

Evangeline smiled and tasted the soup. The deer meat added a richness that balanced the earthiness of the vegetables. She also tasted oregano. The previous villagers must have left some behind.

"This is wonderful," said Evangeline. "I like it much better than what you were making with all the fancy imported ingredients back in the Zoo."

"Thank you," said Angie, her face brightening. "We've been working hard, trying to make do with few ingredients."

"I love it."

She went back to the table and the plant books to finish the soup. It felt good to have a purpose again. A direction for her energy and her life. She smiled for the first time in a very long time.

Tonight would be an introduction to defense. She'd need to start slowly. Some of these people hadn't taken care of their bodies. Just used them to do work. She'd start off with stretching and breathing exercises. And give them a long talk about attitude. Do some strength work and sparring. Give them a couple of easy moves. One to disable an attacker. Another to disarm. End with more stretching. Keep it short and light. None of them were used to physical violence from another human. She'd increase the lessons as everyone grew stronger.

Evangeline hoped they'd all be spared violence from the upcoming war, but that was far beyond her control.

19

CADY

CADY PULLED A FEW WEEDS IN HER SMALL HERB GARDEN and planted a few more mustard seeds for greens. It had rained again last night and soil smelled damp and rich. The greens might make it through the winter, might not. There were never any guarantees with nature. Or with life, for that matter.

Her mind was intent on trying to understand Kali's presence at her window that morning. She hadn't told Beth or Mazzy about the deity. Most people didn't know who Kali was. If they did, they only knew her as Kali, the Destroyer. They didn't know her as the Mother. She embodied both forms.

Which aspect was she embodying now?

Mazzy had gone to spread the word that there would be a meeting tonight. To discuss magic. Cady was not looking forward to it. It was likely Beth would lose her husband tonight. Which the woman seemed to be looking forward to.

Cady had seen it before. Beth was spoiling for a fight, having been passive too long. She had passed any point of reconciliation and was out for blood and revenge.

Cady stood, looking at her small garden. It was a start. If everything went well, she'd have carrots and greens for the fall, and perhaps through the winter. She'd been given potatoes, winter squash, onions and apples and had put them on a table down in the small, hopefully waterproof, root cellar beneath her house. She would add more vegetables to her garden next spring. It would be a lean winter for everyone.

She dusted off her hands and went inside the house. Monster was sleeping on her bed. Cady washed up and ate a bunch of blackberries she'd picked earlier, along with some goat cheese from Joe, her former neighbor. Her meal done, she set off for the Commons.

The Commons was a large wooden building that held everyone in the village, children included, and still had more room. There weren't enough handmade chairs for everyone just yet, but there would be. There was only one room in the building and it was crowded. The new wood walls smelled like the fir used to build them. That scent mingled with the sweat of everyone around. The entire village was working hard to survive.

There was a high counter at one end and behind that, a sink, stove, two large refrigerators and a chest freezer. All scavenged and refurbished by Will and Ryan. The idea was that people would bring their excess food to the Commons and leave them. Those in need could take what was there.

Cady moved to sit in a seat on the edge, but Mazzy and Sharine motioned for her to come up to the center of the circle, near them. Cady sighed and walked through the ring of chairs, three rows deep.

She sat in an empty wood chair, running her hands over the sides of the seat. Even though it was new, the wood felt smooth as glass. Someone had taken their time with this one.

When everyone was present, Mazzy spoke.

"We have two things to talk about tonight. One is the name for our village. We'll save that for last. First, I want to talk about the increase of magic in our village since we moved here to the lake."

There was laughter from several people in the back of the room.

"Magic doesn't exist," said someone behind Cady. A woman's voice.

"It most certainly does," said Joe, who'd never had any powers. He stood slowly, leaning on a carved wood cane. His arthritis must be bothering him. He rubbed his grizzled white beard which stood out in contrast to his blue black skin.

"I've got things happening to me that can't be explained any other way," he said.

"Can you tell us about it Joe?" asked Mazzy.

"Well, you all know I never had any magic, back at the old place. Gave a side eye to those of you who claimed you did, even though I like you well enough. But since we got here, strange things been happening. Every time I turn around I've been seeing Orisha Oko. He's making sure the water's pure. Checking over my goats, helping heal their injuries. Keeping tabs on their kids born this spring. Weeding my crops. He don't talk to me, but I can put my hand right through him. Yesterday, he helped me find one of the babies what had been lost. Led me right to her. She was stuck five feet up in a maple clump, silly thing. Those are only a few of the strange things been happenin'. I could go on all day." Joe dropped down on his chair with a thunk.

"Me too," said Gia, standing and tucking her long dark, hair behind her ears to straighten it. "I've never had any magic either, although I knew other people did. I wasn't able to bring many books with me from our old village, so I haven't had much to do since we got here. I've been helping other people out where I'm able. Every single person I've helped has been having some sort of magical experience. Many of them won't talk about it here. They're too shy or they don't really understand it. People are seeing deities, where they've never been able to before. They're able to heal animals. Where someone's cooking was once awful, they suddenly can now create delicious food. One person is able to be absolutely accurate with what the weather will be for the next two weeks. Another can say beforehand, where the good hunting is and how many of what creature they will catch. Still others can hear their child's thoughts. I think being in this place has something to do with all the magic happening."

There was a lot of noise from the back of the room. Behind Cady. She twisted around to look. It was Liam. Might as well get this over with.

Cady stood to speak.

"Ever since we got here, strange things have been happening. There are a lot of spirits, deities and mythological creatures in this area, for some reason. I don't know why, perhaps the lake is a magnet for them. Magic fills the air. Everywhere I look, one of you has a new-found gift. Some of you haven't noticed yet, or perhaps you just chalked it up as a coincidence. This magic will change our village. We will need to find a way to train people to use their gifts wisely. And we'll need to know which person to call for help with any given problem. Especially in emergencies."

Liam laughed out loud.

"Do you have something to say to all of us Liam?" asked Cady, with as much kindness as she could manage.

He was pacing around the edge of the circle. If any of

them were going to disagree outright, it was him. The big bully.

Finally, he stopped and said, "This is all garbage. Best I can figure is that those of you who are sick, who think you have magic, are poisoning all the others in the village. I think we should never have come here. We should have stayed put. Or maybe those who fancy themselves as having magic to look important, should leave."

"No one is keeping you here," said Mazzy.

"I shouldn't have to leave. You're the ones who are sick."

Mazzy stood, hands on her hips. "You're the one protesting the changes that have happened here. This goes for anyone else here. For some reason, this lake is a magnet for magic. It's only going to increase. If any of you aren't willing to accept that, and the fact that your neighbors, and perhaps even yourself, are going to develop strange powers, then this is the time to pack up and go back to the old village. We will miss you."

Sam stood and said, "There's a problem with that. Our old village has been taken over by people fleeing the Zoo. They've moved in. If you go back, you need to be aware of that."

Liam said, "I'm leaving. Who's with me?"

There was silence. Then Mason, Liam's good buddy, said, "I'm going."

No one else said a word. Cady felt the tension in the room, thick and oppressive like a thundercloud about to shoot down lightening at any moment. She took a deep breath, trying to dissipate her own edginess.

Liam turned to leave the building and said, "C'mon Beth. We're going."

Beth stood in front of her children and said, "I'm staying here. So are the kids."

Liam looked at her and said, "Like hell you are. You're my wife. You come with me."

"No," she said. "I've got magic and so do all the kids. We belong here."

Liam made a move towards her, but Tank and Mateo stepped in front of Beth.

"You can't stop me from taking what's mine."

"This is a free village. No one belongs to anyone else," said Tank.

Tank just crossed his arms and cocked his head at Liam. Liam was a big man, but Tank was huge and muscled. Liam was soft, all fat.

Mateo also stared at Liam, waiting. He was smaller, but wiry and quick. He could use a knife and had one on his hip. Cady wouldn't have wanted to tangle with either Tank or Mateo. Liam, she probably could have taken, back in her prime.

Finally, Liam turned to leave with Mason.

"Damn witch, you can keep her. Not worth anything anyway," he said, spitting on the floor as he left.

The door slammed and they were gone.

Cady caught a movement out of the corner of her eye. She turned to see Kali, dancing outside the window. Destruction, that was the aspect she must be embodying. Or perhaps it was the Mother. The village had protected Beth and her kids.

Beth was openly crying, Cady guessed it was from relief. Sarah handed her baby to Sam and went to Beth, putting her arms around her.

"Thank you all," sobbed Beth.

Beth's kids hugged their Mom and Sarah. One big group hug.

"Well, that settles that," said Mazzy. "I think the name of our village is Enchanted Lake."

"I second that," said Joe.

"I third that," said Beth. "Let's vote."

Mazzy said, "All for it?"

Hands raised in the air.

"All against?"

There were no hands up.

"Passed. Our village is now called Enchanted Lake."

Gia stood and said, "I think Cady's right. We need to talk about how to teach people to use their magic wisely. And organize information about who can do what. Those of you who are interested meet here tomorrow evening after dinner. We'll try to figure out how that might work."

Cady decided to participate. She had some ideas about things. People mingled around and talked. Not yet wanting to leave.

"Fire," yelled Joaquin, running from the window to the door.

Several adults ran after him.

In the growing dusk, Cady could see Beth's house ablaze. There was no question about what happened. Liam had torched the place. Mason didn't have enough imagination, he always followed Liam's lead. Everyone moved out the door, adults corralling the kids.

The wind was blowing. There was no saving Beth's house. People grabbed any container that would hold water and drenched nearby houses. What had Liam used to make the fire spread so quickly? That house had been made of green wood, built not more than a month ago.

Then Cady felt a tingle down her back, the one she always felt when there was big magic going on.

There, standing out in the open was the slight form of Bao. His long, black silken hair swirled in the wind. His eyes were closed and his arms held high, as if calling something.

Cady could see blue streaks of energy coming from his fingers. A dark cloud overhead answered and rain began to fall. Light at first, then a downpour.

It wasn't long before the fire was out.

Cady began to clap. Then the others looked to see what she was clapping about and joined her. Bao dropped his arms and looked around, then down at the ground.

"Are you the reason it's been raining every night?" Cady asked him.

He nodded.

"Is this a new power for you?"

"Yes. I wanted to keep my seeds and seedlings watered, but still have the sun and heat during the day," he said. "There's not much time before the fall rains come."

"Thank you," said Beth.

Beth's house was gone. A charred, smoking mess.

There came a thunder of wings and Onyx landed.

"The man who began the fire and his friend are on the other side of the hill. Running away. Back to your old village. Do you want me to do anything about that?" the dragon asked Cady.

"Bring them back and make them build a new house for Beth," said one voice.

"Good riddance," said Joe.

"Let them go," said Beth. "I never want to see him again."

"There could be consequences," said Sam. "He could lead the people from the Zoo to us."

"Could or will?" asked Cady. "Have you seen something?"

"It's unclear," said Sam. "Every time I try to look into our future here, it's all jumbled. I'm worried."

"I'm unclear too, Sam," said Cady. "I don't trust Morrigu. She's our biggest problem. If Liam and Mason join her, there's no end to the trouble they could bring us."

"What can we do about it? Should I ask Onyx to bring them here?" asked Sam.

"No. We're well rid of them. We'll wait and adapt. We're good at that. I'm not as young and flexible as I once was, but I can change. So can the rest of us. We'll deal with whatever comes by sticking together."

Beth and her children were moved in to Sarah's house, until another house could be built for them.

Several people came up to Cady and Mazzy to tell them they'd be at the meeting tomorrow night to see if they could find a way to teach people how to use their magic. The future of the village looked luminous and filled Cady with hope.

But tonight, tonight was for being grateful that the village had a home. That all of them were safe. That they agreed to accept each other's magic and work together.

Cady gave a deep sigh and thanked the spirits for everything that had come to pass, the good as well as the bad. Everything was a gift.

* * *

Morrigu's Army Grows ...

Damon struggles to build an army for Morrigu. A deluge of new recruits overwhelms him, threatening his hold over the warriors.

Cady and the other villagers find their new home at Enchanted Lake brings surprises. Magic floods into their lives.

Their stories continue to weave tighter and tighter, pulling the two disparate groups together.

Readers of epic fantasy, don't miss this inventive and earthy book as the story pulls us on to the next one.

Islands of Seattle, Book 2

Explosive Resistance: Islands of Seattle, Book 2

ABOUT THE AUTHOR

Linda Jordan writes fascinating characters, visionary worlds, and imaginative fiction. She creates both long and short fiction, serious and silly. She believes in the power of healing and transformation, and many of her stories follow those themes.

In a previous lifetime, Linda coordinated the Clarion West Writers' Workshop as well as the Reading Series. She spent four years as Chair of the Board of Directors during Clarion West's formative period. She's also worked as a travel agent, a baker, and a pond plant/fish sales person, you know, the sort of things one does as a writer.

Currently, she's the Programming Director for the Writers Cooperative of the Pacific Northwest.

Linda now lives in the rainy wilds of Washington state with her husband, daughter, four cats, a cluster of Koi and an infinite number of slugs and snails.

Her other work includes:
Faerie Unraveled, The Bones of the Earth Series, Book 1
Notes on the Moon People
Falling Into Flight
The Black Opal, The Jeweled Worlds Series, Book 1
All her work can be found at your favorite online bookseller.

Get a FREE ebook!

Sign up for Linda's Serendipitous Newsletter at her website: www.LindaJordan.net

Visit her at: www.LindaJordan.net
She can be found on Facebook at:
www.facebook.com/LindaJordanWriter
Metamorphosis Press website is at:
www.MetamorphosisPress.com
Goodreads: https://www.goodreads.com/author/show/2021274.Linda_Jordan

Writers love reviews, even short, simple ones and honest reviews help other readers find the book. Please go to where you bought this book or Goodreads, and leave a review. It would be much appreciated.

Made in the USA
Middletown, DE
26 February 2023